BROKEN DREAMS

A CALLIPUR MURDER MYSTERY

BROKEN DREAMS
A CALLIPUR
MURDER MYSTERY

Aditya Banerjee

Copyright © 2020 Aditya Banerjee

All rights reserved.

Book: 978-1-7773578-1-8
Ebook: 978-1-7773578-0-1

To my father, who always enjoyed a good mystery

Table of Contents

Introduction · ix

1 The Apprentice · · · · · · · · · · · · · · · · · · 1
2 The Recruit · 11
3 The Intern · 26
4 The Journalist · · · · · · · · · · · · · · · · · · 47
5 The Lawyer · 63
6 The Robbery · · · · · · · · · · · · · · · · · · · 84
7 The Club · 109
8 Monsoon · 128
9 Sahibganj · 148
10 Callipur · 170
11 Diwali · 192

About the Author · · · · · · · · · · · · · · · · · 213

Introduction

This murder mystery is set in the town of Callipur in India in 1978. This was well before the age of the internet, mobile phones, surveillance cameras, and advances in forensic technologies. It was the age of rotary phones, manual telephone exchanges, and newspapers. Most Indian households did not have access to television. There was only one television channel, and the only broadcaster was the government. Only a handful of cities in India had access to the broadcast. Callipur was not one of them.

This was also a time when most people trusted the news they read in the papers. All Indians got their news from the newspapers and the radio. It was also the year after the "Emergency" period in India ended. The "Indian Emergency" was a period of upheaval and shock for its citizens. This period eroded India's trust in its government. It was a period when its civil liberties were suspended, and a time of fear and unrest that led to a number of arrests and atrocities against innocent people. It also had a profound impact on the police and judiciary.

By 1978, democracy had been restored, although the general distrust in the government remained. Callipur was an affluent midsize town on the east coast on the Bay of Bengal. It held India's promise of a new, modern, and industrial nation that was desperately trying to break free of the shackles of a bygone era. It represented the promise and potential of a new generation of Indians in all walks of life. This is the backdrop of the story and the events that unfolded that year. A horrific slaying forced the establishment to find justice. It also challenged some of the people involved in the case to confront long-held ideals and societal norms.

1

The Apprentice

The Bhaskar brothers ran the Callipur Auto Shop. They had inherited the business from their father. It was well managed, and the brothers made sure that the company was profitable.

Praveen Bhaskar, the older of the two brothers, invested all his time and resources in the shop. It had been almost a decade since his wife had died, and his only daughter was married and living in Delhi. She had shown no interest in the business or coming back to settle in Callipur. Praveen knew that at some point he would have to sell his share of the business to his brother.

Since his daughter's departure, he had found himself spending even more time at the shop. He had converted a small room in the top floor to a makeshift rest area for himself. There was a small cot and a sofa, ideal for an afternoon nap. His only vice was the bottle. He loved drinking. There was a time when he used to drink only in the club. But in the past few months, he had started drinking at home and in the shop after closing for the day.

His younger brother, Pramod, was worried about his drinking habit. Twice in the last six months, Pramod had found Praveen passed out and sleeping at night in the small room upstairs, and Pramod had to help get him back home. He had confronted Praveen, and his brother had politely told him to mind his own business.

Pramod Bhaskar was the more ambitious one. He had left town for a few years and had recently returned to take up his stake in the family business. His father had sent him to Calcutta for higher studies, hoping that he would learn some new skills and make some headway in finding new business opportunities. He had gotten involved in a few ventures, but eventually, they all fizzled out. Pramod had also looked into whether their business could be expanded with another workshop in the neighboring town of Sahibganj. But that did not go anywhere, either.

Now he was back, firmly settled in the family business. He liked his older brother and looked up to him. He was also thankful that Praveen had kept the business running while he was away and did not make much of a fuss when he returned. He knew that his niece was not interested in the auto shop and that eventually he would have to buy out his brother's share. His wife, Radhika, was coaxing him to get that done sooner rather than later for the sake of their son, Amit. Amit was still in high school. He was an intelligent boy who had shown even less of an interest in the shop. But he was a boy, and this was the family business. From Pramod's standpoint, his son's lack of interest was not a concern. It just delayed the inevitable.

The Bhaskars hired good people, paid them a fair wage, and treated them well. They invested in the latest tools and machinery. There was not much by way of competition inside Callipur. The only other auto shops were in gas stations in the outskirts that catered mostly to heavier vehicles. Business was good. Their workshop was big. The building was located in a gated compound that the brothers owned. The ground floor contained a large, covered area that could easily service six or seven cars at a time. The top floor was smaller. It had offices for the brothers, a small rest area, a large hall with a few desks, and typewriters for the clerks who performed all the accounting and secretarial duties. There was also a storage room that mostly housed old equipment. On any given day, there were anywhere between three to five cars in the garage. There were eight full-time mechanics who worked on the ground floor and three clerks on the top floor. The brothers usually stayed in their offices.

When Karan Lal had shown up a few weeks earlier to ask for an apprentice position, both the brothers were a bit surprised. They knew Karan's father, Professor Saumya Lal. The Lals were relative newcomers to Callipur. Saumya had retired from a private school in a nearby town and had moved to Callipur. From what they had heard at the club, this was mainly to be near the hospital for getting treatment for an underlying heart condition. Saumya had an old Fiat that he'd brought to the shop for service and maintenance. The brothers knew that the professor was a good man, well liked with a good sense of humor. They had also seen him in the club a few times, and their interactions with him had always been pleasant and cordial.

So, when the professor's son showed up at the garage, their first question was whether his father approved of Karan working in the auto shop. Pramod was talking to some of the workers on the shop floor when Karan showed up.

"Is Mr. Lal aware of this?"

"Yes."

"You just graduated from high school this year. Correct?"

"Yes."

"Why aren't you applying for college?"

"I have decided to chart my own course."

"And what is that?"

"I am interested in cars. I want to learn how to fix them."

"And after that?" Pramod smiled and was now curious to know what this boy was thinking.

"I want to save some money. After a few years, I want to move to a big city and have my own workshop."

"What does your father think of this plan?"

Karan thought carefully. "Initially, he wasn't happy with the idea of me not going to college. But I managed to convince him that college is not something I want to do. I want to learn a trade and start something. I want to build something on my own."

Pramod could only imagine how the conversation must have gone with the professor. How difficult that must have been. He was impressed by the boy's ambition. He wondered whether Amit or his niece would ever show this sort of initiative. He looked Karan straight in the eye.

"You do realize that we have to talk to your father and make sure that he is OK with this?"

"I understand."

"I also have to talk to my brother. In fact, he is upstairs. Let's go have a word with him now."

As they climbed the stairs, Karan could see the cars that had come in for repairs and servicing. There was a Jeep, two Ambassadors and a Fiat. He could see the mechanics huddled around them with all sorts of tools and oils. When they reach the top floor, he saw the clerks in the hallway and heard the clickety-clack sound of the typewriters. He smiled as he walked past them to the end of the large room. Through a glass barrier, he could see Praveen Bhaskar talking to someone on the phone. They waited outside until Praveen hung up.

"This is Karan Lal. Professor Saumya's son," Pramod introduced him.

"Yes. I know. He has come here with his father to drop off the car a few times. How are you, Karan? How is your father? Everything good with the Fiat?"

"Yes, sir."

"He wants to join our workshop as an apprentice," Pramod said.

Praveen had the same puzzled look on his face. He turned to Karan.

"Your father's OK with this?" He rehashed the entire conversation that Karan had had with Pramod on the shop floor a few minutes earlier.

"Well, I don't see a problem. Our mechanics are all getting old. It would be good to have some new blood. If you are good, you should be able to get a full-time role in a few months. You have to show up on time and work hard."

Karan was happy. He smiled and nodded in agreement. He thanked them profusely.

"Let me talk to the professor later today. If he agrees, you can start next week."

Karan left. Praveen called the professor and made sure that he had his approval for his son to join as an apprentice. He could sense that the professor was not too happy about it but had eventually relented to his son's wishes.

Karan stepped out of the workshop onto the path leading to the gates exiting the compound a few hundred yards away. He was extremely pleased with himself. He recalled the several heated conversations he'd had with his father after his high school exam. In a country where everyone saw education as a ticket to a better job and life in the government or industry, he had decided to forgo that for a career in the trades and start his own business. It was all the more embarrassing for a professor's son to not go to college. Callipur was still a small town. Everyone would talk about this and view this as a failure not only for Karan but also for the professor. There would be talk about how the professor could not bring up his son properly and help him academically. The irony was not lost on Karan. But he stood his ground, and after many, many hours of discussions and arguments, he was able to convince his father.

Saumya was a mild-mannered gentleman, well read, well liked, and spent his time either in his books at home or in the library at the club. His wife had died when Karan was young. He had taken up a job in a private school in Sahibganj. Karan was able to study at the same school and excelled in sports and extracurricular activities. He had always shown an interest in cars, but the professor thought that was a passing phase. He never realized that his son would consider it as a profession. He also never thought that Karan would not be going to college. But once the high school exams were over, Karan had approached him with the idea. Initially, he had dismissed it completely. He tried very hard to make his son understand the value of higher education and the doors that it would open. Being an only parent, he had no one else to help him influence his son. He was close to Karan. He knew that his son was not strong academically. His school exams would probably get him into a college with a modest reputation somewhere, but not any premier institution. Karan, for his part, had made a passionate plea and compelling arguments for his decision.

Eventually, Saumya had relented. His agreement was conditional. Karan would start as an apprentice. If he did not like it, then he would have to find a way to get himself admitted to college. He would lose a year compared to his friends. But Saumya knew that in the grand scheme of things that was not important. He also knew that Karan was a responsible kid who had made so many little sacrifices to ensure that his father was in good health and getting the best treatment for his failing heart.

Karan had inherited his father's pleasant and amicable disposition. Everyone had something nice to say about him. His teachers knew that he tried hard, and although he did not get good grades, he never got into trouble at school. He had a good circle of friends. When he arrived in Callipur from Sahibganj, he had two more years of school left. He was able to adjust and quickly make friends and signed up for extracurricular activities. He was also able to find time to take care of his father. He made sure that Saumya had a routine, registered him with the club library, and established a good rapport with the doctors at the hospital treating his father's heart condition.

Karan was happy with how things had turned out. He knew that the job at the auto shop involved long hours. But this was something he wanted. He loved cars and everything about them. He was eager to please the Bhaskar brothers and prove to his dad that he could make it.

He was off to a good start. The workers in the shop liked him. He was a fast learner and dedicated worker. The owners were impressed by his work ethic. Even the professor was happy that his son was enjoying his new job.

It was a shock to everyone when Karan was found brutally slain on a late spring night in the workshop just a few weeks after he had started working there.

2

The Recruit

When the phone rang that night, Shankar Sen was the officer on duty at the police station. He had arrived for his posting three months ago. He was a new graduate from the police academy. Like most people in town who worked in the steel plant, the paper mill, or the port, he was not from Callipur. He grew up in Dehradun, a town in the foothills of the Himalayas. His only foray into coastal India and the Bay of Bengal, where Callipur was located, was during one of the very few vacations his family could afford when he was a teenager. They had traveled to a coastal fishing village a hundred miles south to visit some extended family members.

Growing up near the mountains, Shankar was not used to the sea and the smell of salt in the air. He did not like the hot and humid weather. But he did like the experience. Callipur was a good posting. The law and order situation was better compared to many other parts of the state or even the country. The town was cosmopolitan. The new industries and port meant that people from all over India came to settle and work there.

Shankar belonged to a different India in other respects, too. He came from a modest but large family. His father worked as a postman, and as a family, they struggled to make ends meet during most of his childhood. He knew that education was his only way out. He was the youngest in his family. His two sisters and brother were settled in Dehradun. They had put themselves through school and college and were happy to find jobs locally that paid a decent living wage. His father had retired. With all the kids out of the house, he was happy to spend his pension catering to his wife's whims and fancies. Their financial situation had slowly improved with Shankar getting into the police service.

Shankar had always been a good student academically and was physically active. His desire to get into the police force came early. One of his uncles who was in the army had told him stories of valor and courage. Shankar was also impressed each time he saw his uncle in uniform. During the 1971 war, when Shankar had just turned fourteen, his uncle had been killed. Nevertheless, Shankar grew up as an idealist. He wanted to join a uniformed service to make a difference. One of his teachers had encouraged him to take the service exams during the final year of his bachelor's program, and he passed them on his first attempt. Passing the physical was never a problem. He was always athletic and liked to run every day. After a year at the academy, he was posted at Callipur. With all the new changes that were made to the service, the prevailing wisdom of the police hierarchy was to place new graduates in regional police stations for a year or two before allocating any extended assignments in bigger cities.

While he enjoyed his time at the academy, his first assignment in the real world was turning out to be a different sort of learning experience. The trainers and teachers at the academy had warned him of different kinds of officers with varying degrees of adherence to procedure and of political interference in investigations. To some extent, he was prepared to see all of that in a big city. But he never imagined that a posting in a relatively modest and peaceful town with a small force would also offer vastly contrasting personalities. His immediate boss was Alok Vij. Alok was well connected politically, had a good pedigree, wanted to get fast results, was socially adept and well spoken, and had a reputation for being a lousy police officer. He spent most of the day and afternoon at the police station and evenings and nights at the Colonial Club. Shankar had quickly learned not to "disturb" him during his evenings at the club and never to make him look bad in front of his superiors. It was rumored that Alok Vij was on his way up, and his transfer to a more prestigious post in Delhi was only a matter of time. "Any day now," colleagues at the club had said.

Shankar felt deflated to see someone like Alok getting plum posts only because of the right connections. From what Shankar had observed over the last three months, tagging along with Alok on different investigations, Alok was in the perception game. He was out to please and never criticized or bad-mouthed anyone. He also did not get much done on cases assigned to him. Yet he managed to insert himself in all high-profile cases and was at the forefront when it came to getting accolades once they were all concluded. *You need talent for that*, Shankar thought. The saving grace was that Alok's boss was Maheshwar Mishra, or Mishra-ji, as everyone seemed to call him, and he was legendary.

Shankar had heard about Maheshwar Mishra at the academy. He had a reputation of sorts, both good and bad on the force and in public. He was known to be an honest, incorruptible officer who delivered results. He was also hotheaded, insubordinate, and foul-mouthed when it came to dealing with his peers and superiors. He had been suspended twice from the force due to using heavy-handed tactics in dealing with crowds. On both occasions, the inquiry commissions had absolved him of any wrongdoing, and he had been reinstated.

Over the years, he had mellowed, but he still maintained a passion for doing the right thing. Given his past suspensions, his superiors had decided to post him in roles not directly involved in tackling unruly crowds. He was a few months away from retiring, and Callipur was his last posting. The commissioner had asked him to take charge of training the new recruits and assigning them to different officers and investigations.

When Shankar showed up, Maheshwar didn't have much of a choice. There was only one other officer who hadn't been assigned a recruit, and that's how Shankar ended up with Alok. Despite that, Maheshwar took a personal interest in all the recruits and would invariably come by their offices once every week to see how they were doing. Shankar respected that.

When Shankar picked up the phone that night, he could hear commotion in the background.

"Hello, is this the police station?" a man asked.

"Yes."

"My name is Pramod Bhaskar. I am calling from the Callipur Auto Shop. We found one of our workers lying on the floor. He seems to have been beaten and is not moving. We think he is dead."

"Have you called the hospital?"

"No. We wanted to call the police station first."

"Call the hospital, and ask them to send an ambulance. Please don't touch or move anything from the scene. I am leaving right away. Most likely, I will be there before the ambulance arrives."

"Malkhan, please bring the Jeep around. We need to leave right away. Callipur Auto Shop."

"Yes, sir." Malkhan, the driver assigned to Shankar, knew exactly where that was.

Shankar looked at his watch. It was nearly 2:00 a.m. The shop was a short drive from the police station. Shankar wondered if this was another robbery attempt gone wrong. There had been a gang of robbers breaking into shops, stores, and factories lately. Several incidents had been reported across the state, mostly in and around Callipur, over the past few weeks. The gang's most recent attempts had become even more brazen. There were a couple of incidents where the guards and owners at these establishments had been beaten.

Broken Dreams: A Callipur Murder Mystery

Police from different jurisdictions had created a task force to tackle this menace. Alok was part of the task force. They had made some headway in the investigation, but they still had not been successful in catching anyone. From what Shankar had heard from his colleagues about apprehending the gang in the last meeting, they thought they were close. Apparently, they had some new leads from an informant but didn't want to share many details. They were worried that someone at the one of the police stations may be tipping off the gang.

He could now see the gates to the compound entrance leading to the garage. The auto shop was a few yards from the gate. Apart from the building that housed the auto shop, there was what looked like a broken shed on one side. The other side contained a small, wooded area with some car parts on the ground. He couldn't see everything clearly and made a mental note to come back during the day. He asked Malkhan to stop right after entering the gates. He walked up the pathway leading to the shop.

The ambulance still hadn't arrived. He could see a group of people huddled in one corner. It was easy to figure out who the owner was.

"Hello, Officer. My name is Pramod Bhaskar. I am one of the owners of this establishment."

"Shankar Sen. Have you called for an ambulance?"

"Yes. They will be arriving shortly."

"Can you show me where the victim is?"

"Right this way." As Pramod let Shankar to where he'd found Karan, the owner was surprised to see such a young police officer being assigned to this. *Maybe a senior officer will be taking over soon*, he thought.

Karan was lying facedown on the floor with a huge gash in the back of his head. Whatever struck him must have been heavy, and whoever did this must have done so with immense strength. There was blood on the floor. Shankar looked around to see if he could find any instrument with any blood on it. He couldn't. He asked Malkhan to cordon off the area where the body was, then fetch the coroner and police photographer. He also asked Pramod and his employees to leave the premises. He instructed them not to enter the building until the next day.

While everyone was outside, Shankar did another survey of the ground floor. Then he stepped outside and headed toward Pramod.

"Who found the body?"

"I did."

"What's the victim's name?"

"Karan Lal. He joined us as an apprentice a few weeks ago."

"Do you know why he was here at this hour?"

"I am not quite sure. You will have to ask the other workers. I usually leave around six p.m., and whoever leaves last locks the garage."

"Was Karan ever the last to leave?"

"Yes. It's never been a problem."

"You left at six p.m. Why did you come back?"

"I was coming back from the movies. And as I was driving past, I saw that the gates were still open. It was around one a.m. Usually, we close around eight. So, I came inside to check, and I found him lying on the floor."

"Where did you go for the movies? Which show?"

"The latest Hitchcock movie that's playing at the Globe."

Shankar could sense that Pramod was starting to get annoyed with all these questions. He didn't care.

"Why did you call your employees to come to the garage when you found the victim?"

"I wanted to know if they knew anything. Or if they could tell me what Karan was doing at the shop at this late hour."

"You said you are one of the owners of this establishment. I am guessing the other one is your brother?"

"Yes."

"Does he know what happened here?"

"Not yet. I haven't told him."

"One last question: Do you have a phone on the premises? I have to make a quick call to my boss."

"Yes. You will have to go upstairs and then all the way to the end of the hall. You will see two offices there. The one on the left, belonging to my brother, has the telephone."

"Thank you."

Shankar waited till Malkhan had returned with the photographer and a doctor who would examine the body. Callipur was a small police station. It didn't have dedicated resources for either but worked with one of the photo store owners and the medical staff in the hospital in such cases. Once the photographer had taken all the pictures, Shankar walked over to the young doctor who was examining the body and introduced himself.

"Shankar Sen. I am sorry to drag you here at this hour, Doctor."

"Daphader."

"Sorry?"

"That's my name. Daphader."

"Oh. Right. So, Dr. Daphader, any insight on what may have happened?"

"Wicked stuff."

"How so?"

"I can't say for sure until we have completed the postmortem, but he seems to have been hit with a blunt object. A single, heavy blow to the back of the head."

"Time of death?"

"At this point, just a guess. I'd say anywhere between ten p.m. and one a.m. We should be able to narrow things down after the postmortem." The doctor finished examining the body.

"If you are done, we can make arrangements to have the body shifted to the hospital."

"Have you notified the next of kin yet?" the doctor asked.

"No."

"Sad, really. Young fellow. Ghastly end. Well, I will be off then. If you want to pass by the hospital tomorrow afternoon, I should have the details of the postmortem."

"Thank you, Doctor."

Before asking the ambulance staff to remove the body, Shankar headed upstairs to Praveen Bhaskar's office to make a quick call to Alok Vij. It was nearly 4:00 a.m. Mrs. Vij picked up the phone sounding understandably sleepy and irritated. She handed the phone to Alok.

"Murder, you say?" Alok asked.

Broken Dreams: A Callipur Murder Mystery

"Yes, sir. Seems that way."

"Hm."

Shankar informed him that the photographer had taken detailed pictures of the crime scene. A doctor from the hospital had examined the body, and he was making arrangements to send the victim for a postmortem that morning.

"Excellent. Good work, Sen."

"I wanted to know if you want to visit the crime scene before they take him away."

There was a momentary silence on the other end of the phone. Then Alok asked, "Who is the victim? Do we know?"

"Yes. Karan Lal. He was an apprentice. He had started here a few weeks ago."

"Family?"

"Father. A retired professor. Saumya Lal."

After what seemed like another prolonged silence, Alok said, "I think it's important to get the postmortem done right away and release the victim's body. We have everything we need from the site. It should be fine."

"Right, sir."

"Let's meet at the station at ten a.m. Who is there with you?"

"Malkhan."

"OK. Call the station. Have them send two guards there to make sure no one disturbs anything at the scene until we have completed our investigation. Also, please inform the poor father."

"Yes, sir." After hanging up, Shankar couldn't help but wonder if Alok's response to visit the scene of crime would have been different if this were a high-profile victim. He called the station, asked them to send the guards, and then stepped outside Praveen Bhaskar's office to head downstairs.

As he left the office, he could smell tobacco and alcohol coming from one of the rooms on the other side of the hallway. He went over, opened the door, and stepped inside. He found three half-empty bottles of whisky on the floor, a small cot with sheets drenched in alcohol and water, and a room in a state of complete disarray. He quickly went to find Malkhan.

"Is the photographer still here?"

"Yes, sir. He is waiting in the car. I told him that we will drop him off on our way back to the station."

"Bring him upstairs. He needs to take a few more pictures."

Shankar made sure that the photographer meticulously took pictures of the small room, the offices of the brothers, the hall where the clerks sat, the stairway, and the storage room. Before leaving, he did a thorough search of the premises with Malkhan. Once the guards arrived, he gave them strict instructions not to let anyone enter the premises. Then he went back to the car and asked Malkhan to drop off the photographer, told the photographer that he needed all the pictures the same day, and then headed to inform professor Saumya of the sad news. He was not looking forward to it.

3

The Intern

When Alok arrived at the police station, Shankar was already in his office and at his desk, finishing up his report about the auto shop.

"Did you even go home? I hope you got some sleep. It will be a long day."

"Yes, sir."

"Good. How did it go with the boy's father?"

"He is completely distraught and heartbroken."

"Understandably so," Alok replied. Shankar could sense that the gravity of the crime was slowly sinking in.

"I left him at the hospital. Some of Karan's friends and parents are helping him with the last rites. Dr.

Daphader, who was at the scene, promised to complete the postmortem first thing this morning and release the body as soon as possible."

Alok nodded and was pleased to hear that.

"Well, the first thing is to head back to the site. We should look over the shop and the surrounding areas for the weapon involved or any evidence. Second, we need written statements from all the employees and the owners regarding their whereabouts and alibis, if they have any."

"Right, sir. Will you be coming with me?"

"Yes. We need some more bodies. The statements will go faster that way. Let's ask Arun and Sanjay to join us. I have already cleared it with Mishra-ji. We can brief them on the way."

Arun and Sanjay were the other new officers in Callipur. They mainly dealt with traffic-related incidents and land disputes. A small station with limited resources meant that everyone had to chip in when needed. They could take statements once they were briefed properly. *It shouldn't be complicated*, Shankar thought.

Once they arrived at the auto shop, the employees were there. The Bhaskar brothers were not. The guards had made the workers wait in a small area just inside the gate on the pathway leading up to the entrance to the garage. They were all visibly shaken and sad. Karan was a new employee but was well liked, and several seemed fearful about whether this would happen again.

Alok instructed Arun and Sanjay to start taking statements. His and Shankar's main focus was to search the compound for the weapon.

"Let's divide this up," Alok said. "I will take the shop floor while you take the second floor, and then we can switch. After that, we can both search the area outside."

A good plan, Shankar thought.

They spent the next four hours searching each floor and the grounds. It was futile. But the thorough search did reveal that there had been someone or several people drinking in the little room on the second floor. Shankar made sure that all the glasses, sheets, and bottles were collected for fingerprint analysis. That would take days. They had to send all evidence to the state capital. There was no lab in Callipur.

While searching the grounds, he and Alok also found tire marks near the shed and some cigarette butts. That seemed to suggest that at some point, someone might have been waiting there. But they were definitely not hiding. The shed was right next to the shop floor entrance on one side, and anyone in the garage could clearly see anything parked in front of it.

Shankar noticed butts and matches on either side of where the vehicle had been, indicating that there were at least two passengers. Unless there were any witnesses, apart from sending the butts for further analysis, this was mostly a dead end. There was nothing to suggest that the tracks were from the night the incident took place. From the width, he concluded that the car was probably an Ambassador. All cars in India in 1978 were either Fiats or Ambassadors, and each had the same brand of tires.

The only other piece of evidence worth noting was something on the outside gate leading into the compound. The paint on the wooden gate on one side was slightly chipped. Perhaps a car nicked it. It would surely have left a mark on one side of the vehicle. A quick survey of all the cars in the shop indicated that it was not one of them. The workers confirmed that the gate had been painted a few weeks ago and that the damage to the gate was recent.

When the officers finished, it was nearly 3:00 p.m. They still needed statements from the brothers. Alok suggested that they head back to the station with everything they had collected and make arrangements for what was needed to be sent off for analysis right away. He skimmed over a couple of statements and was satisfied with the details. He handed some to Shankar, who quickly glanced at them and nodded in agreement.

Alok and Shankar had to head back to the station. There was an important meeting to discuss the security arrangements at the steel plant. The labor union at the steel plant had called for a strike over the weekend and that meant that the entire police department would be tied up in maintaining law and order in and around the plant. Alok instructed the other officers to go to the Bhaskars' residence to get their statements.

Before leaving, Alok asked, "Have we covered everything?"

Shankar thought for a moment and then turned to one of the workers who seemed to be the leader of the pack. "Do you keep an inventory of all the tools in the shop?"

"Yes. But it's not always up-to-date or accurate. There is a register."

"Can you please check if anything's missing?"

"That would take hours. We have a lot of tools."

"I understand. But it might help in catching who did this to your colleague. One other thing. Do you have a list of all the cars that have been serviced here?"

"Yes. But that would be a lot of cars. How far back do you want us to go?"

"When did Karan start?"

"About eight weeks ago."

"The last eight weeks then. Thank you," Shankar said.

"We will get on it and let you know by tomorrow. Can we go back inside now?"

Shankar looked at Alok, who shrugged and said, "I don't see why not. Our work here is done. If we need anything else, we can always come back."

As the workers filed back into the shop, there was still no sign of the Bhaskar brothers.

When they arrived back at the station, Maheshwar called Alok and Shankar to his office for a full update. Shankar was mostly quiet during the meeting and answered only when asked. He sensed from the discussion that Alok was trying to link the killing to the gang responsible for the string of robberies in the area.

"Do you know, sir, that the gang had targeted the same garage a few weeks ago?"

"Really?" Maheshwar was curious.

"Yes. I checked that this morning. Praveen Bhaskar had filed a report."

"You think they wanted to hit it again? Was there anything missing this time?"

"Well, we have asked that they check their inventory and let us know," Alok said. Shankar was both impressed and surprised by how smoothly he did that.

"All right. Please keep me posted of any new developments. Meanwhile the strike at the steel plant takes priority this weekend," Maheshwar said. He did not want a repeat of what happened a few months ago during the last labor unrest. There were a few skirmishes between the workers and the police with a few injuries. This time around they had called in reinforcements from neighboring towns and had cordoned off a large area outside the plant with barricades to ensure that the protest was peaceful.

As they were leaving, Maheshwar called out, "Oh, Alok, I forgot to mention. Nitya is waiting for you in your office. She wants a statement for the paper about the incident this morning. She was here following up on the robberies case and then learned about this."

"Sure, Mishra-ji. I will take care of it."

As they turned into the corridor leading to Alok's office, Alok said, "Come along. I will introduce you to Nitya. She is a reporter from *The Callipur Post*."

"Sure, sir."

As they reached the end of the corridor, Shankar could see her waiting outside the office. He had seen her before in the club a few times but hadn't known who she was.

"Hello, Nitya. How are you?" Alok said.

"Good afternoon, Alok," Nitya replied.

"Come, let's sit." Alok led them inside his office.

Once they were seated, Nitya looked at Shankar, stretched out her hand, and said, "I am Nitya Chaturvedi from *The Callipur Post*."

"Shankar Sen."

"He is one of our new recruits. He is assigned to me and helping me with the case."

"Splendid," she replied. "What can you tell the people of Callipur so far? Is this death related to the robberies? Do the people need to be worried?"

"Come, come, Nitya. You know we cannot answer those questions less than a day into the investigation. Yes, it could be linked to the robberies, but we are still trying to ascertain that," Alok said.

Unbelievable, Shankar thought. Alok didn't want to answer the question and yet answered it anyway. Nitya looked at Shankar, who was visibly withdrawn. His body language suggested that he did not agree with his boss. Nitya pressed Alok further.

"Do you need any help from the press? Any request for help from the general population?"

"Not at this time," Alok replied. "We must really get moving on this. Let's meet and catch up at the club."

"Sure." She got up to leave.

"Please give my regards to your parents, and say hi to Raj."

"Will do," Nitya replied and left the room.

Alok turned to Shankar and smiled. "That's Mrs. Chaturvedi's daughter."

Shankar had no idea what that meant. Wasn't she Mr. Chaturvedi's daughter, too? And who was Raj? Her husband? Fiancé? He refused to engage further with Alok on this.

"Let's go to our meeting. Hopefully, it won't take long. We can then grab some lunch and head over to the hospital to get the postmortem report," Alok said. Shankar nodded in agreement.

At the hospital, they discovered there had been a row over the report between Dr. Rohit Daphader and his immediate supervisor, Dr. Arora, who was also the coroner. The postmortem had been completed. They had to share the findings with the police and then get their permission to release the body to Lal's family.

As Alok and Shankar walked towards Dr. Arora's office, they could see the boy's father, some of his friends, and others huddled on the other side. Callipur General was a fairly modern and new hospital. It was the only hospital in town. It was also big. The government and the local companies that had invested in it had made sure that it could cater to the expanding needs of the town's population and industries. Having a steel plant, a paper mill, and a port within a fifty-kilometer radius meant that a hospital had to be equipped to handle any large incident. And it was. It had also managed to attract doctors and specialists from all over India. The staff were well taken care of, and there was a healthy rotation of interns that transferred through the hospital. That's where Dr. Daphader came in. He had already finished his medical degree in Delhi and was specializing in surgery. As part of his specialization, he was interning at the hospital. His supervisor in Delhi had recommended Callipur since it was a new hospital with new, modern infrastructure.

Rohit Daphader came from a family of doctors. His father was a doctor. His grandfather was a doctor. He was also married to someone whose father was also a doctor. The difference was that his father in-law had his own private practice mainly catering to the rich and famous in Delhi while his own father was a government doctor. Rohit had always been a good student. He had secured grades good enough to get him into one of the top-ranked medical colleges in Delhi. He had met Smita during one of the many Indian festivals. They were both studying at the time. She was pursuing a degree in political science at a different college. It was a fast courtship, and the families had decided that they should get married as soon as possible. Smita's father was on the lookout for a son in-law who was a doctor so that he could pass on his practice to him. He was ecstatic when he learned that his only daughter was interested in marrying Rohit. That was almost two years ago.

Rohit jumped at the opportunity. He wanted to move out of Delhi. Both his parents and in-laws were making life difficult for him and Smita. They felt an overbearing need to barge into every decision that the couple tried to make. Their extended family and friends didn't help, either. There were constant questions and remarks about when they were going to start a family, when Rohit would be joining his father in-law's practice, whether Smita would be working, and so on.

No one knew Smita and Rohit in Callipur. They were quite social at the club and had managed to make some new friends. There were plenty of people from Delhi in Callipur as well. They could reminisce with them when they wanted and then move on.

Rohit was a good doctor. His only flaw was that he could come across as being cocky and arrogant when dealing with others. It didn't matter who it was: his peers, his superiors, or other staff at the hospital. But in the few months that he had been at Callipur General, he had made a name for himself as a knowledgeable, studious, and able doctor.

When the phone rang early in the morning, he was the one on night duty. It had been a busy night. Once he had finished at the auto shop, he came back to the hospital and made some meticulous notes. He called his supervisor, Dr. Arora, to let him know what had happened. He also obtained his approval to do the postmortem. Being an intern, he couldn't sign off on the final report. He could only be a cosignatory.

He was happy to see the familiar face of Shankar Sen walking toward him while he was engaged in an argument with his supervisor. Once the two officers introduced themselves, everyone went into Dr. Arora's office. The postmortem report was straightforward. The gist of it, as the officers had presumed, was that a single heavy blow from a blunt instrument at the back of the head was responsible for the poor boy's death. It had occurred sometime between 11:00 p.m. and midnight. From the tone of the conversation, it was apparent that Dr. Arora and Alok knew each other quite well.

"Were there any defensive injuries? Anything to indicate a fight or physical altercation?" Shankar asked.

"Not particularly. We analyzed his fingernails to check for tissue. It was mostly grease. Not surprising, given that he worked in an auto shop."

Broken Dreams: A Callipur Murder Mystery

"Anything to suggest that he was intoxicated or using drugs?" Alok asked.

"No," Dr. Arora replied.

He handed over the report to Alok, who took a quick look at it, made sure that it had the coroner's signature, and passed into Shankar, who started reading it.

"Can we release the body to the family now?" Dr. Daphader asked.

"I don't see why not," Alok replied.

"I will get you to sign off on the paperwork," Dr. Arora replied. "Please come with me." As Arora and Alok left the room, both Shankar and Dr. Daphader sensed that they wanted to talk about something privately.

Shankar was still reading the report. He slowly got up, turned to Dr. Daphader, pointed in Alok and Dr. Arora's direction, and asked, "Do they know each other?"

"Yes. Buddies at the club."

As they left the room and entered the corridor, they saw Nitya talking to the family of the boy.

"Isn't that the reporter from *The Callipur Post?*"

"Yes. That's Nitya," Dr. Daphader replied. "She has an interest in the case, too. I saw her talking to Dr. Arora before you showed up."

"If you don't mind my asking, what were you and Dr. Arora arguing about? Anything to do with the case?"

"Yes."

Shankar could sense that he had hit a nerve.

The young doctor looked at Shankar and said, "For whatever reason, he wanted me to write in the report that there was no conclusive evidence to determine whether there was an altercation. My statement was that based on the physical evidence, there wasn't. He didn't want such a definitive remark. I refused to change the initial statement. I told him he could do it himself, and he did. I was arguing with him about that when you came by."

"Interesting," Shankar said. He wondered if Alok and Dr. Arora had spoken about the case before he and Alok had arrived.

"Usually, we get one or two emergencies a night, minor things from the plant if there's a night shift. But yesterday, there was nothing from the plant, the mill, or the port. That auto shop kept me busy. First, we had to deal with the fellow who was drunk and passed out. Then we took the call about the poor boy who was killed."

Shankar suddenly stopped walking. He recalled the little room on the second floor of the garage, the empty bottles, the bedsheets drenched in alcohol. He turned to the doctor, his tone suddenly serious.

"So, you dealt with two emergencies from the same shop that night?"

"Yes. The drunk fellow who showed up at the emergency room last night was also from the same garage."

"Is he still in the hospital?"

"No. We released him this morning." Dr. Daphader wondered whether he should have mentioned that earlier.

"He spent the night here?" Shankar asked.

"Yes."

"What time did he come in?"

"I saw him around ten p.m. He must have come in a few minutes earlier."

"Who brought him in?" Shankar asked.

"His brother. I saw him at the shop last night. He is the co-owner of the same garage."

"The gentleman you treated is Praveen Bhaskar? His brother, Pramod Bhaskar, is the one who brought him in?"

"Yes."

"Thank you, Doctor."

Shankar was lost in thought. He didn't see that Nitya had suddenly appeared by his side.

"Hello, Rohit. Shankar."

"Hi, Nitya," Dr. Daphader replied.

"Good afternoon, Nitya-ji," Shankar said.

"Anything to add for my readers regarding this sad incident?" she asked Shankar.

"No," Shankar replied.

"No connection between Praveen Bhaskar being injured the same night his apprentice is killed in his workshop?" Nitya pressed further.

Shankar was surprised she knew this but kept his composure. "No."

"I will leave you to it, then. I am going to the boy's cremation. I would imagine Alok and you will be there, too, Shankar?"

"Yes," he replied.

As she walked away, Dr. Daphader recalled that he had seen Dr. Arora speaking with Nitya earlier. *He must have told her about Praveen Bhaskar*, Shankar thought.

Shankar saw Alok waving from end of the corridor with a report in his hand. It was time for them to leave.

"Dr. Daphader, thank you for all your help. You have given us a lot to think about, and I really appreciate the prompt postmortem report."

"You are most welcome. Do you visit the club?"

"Sometimes."

"Please come by more often. I am sure we can talk about other things as well."

"Sure."

They shook hands, and Shankar hurried to get to the hospital gates where Alok was waiting for him. He wanted to let him know about Praveen Bhaskar's visit to the hospital shortly before they'd been called to the shop. But as he approached Alok, he could see that Alok was distant.

"I need to get back to the station. Something to do with the robberies. It seems there is some new evidence that might break open the case, and someone from the task force is here. I have to go meet them right away at the station."

"Right, sir."

"I will ask Malkhan to drop me off at the station, and you can go to the boy's last rites."

"Yes, sir," Shankar said, then added, "Dr. Daphader told me that Praveen Bhaskar was treated at the hospital last night. His brother had brought him a little before ten p.m. He was drunk and delirious. He was released this morning."

Broken Dreams: A Callipur Murder Mystery

"Doesn't quite fit the timeline, does it?" Alok looked at Shankar and continued. "The report says that the boy was killed between eleven p.m. and midnight. But the Bhaskars were already here at ten."

"Yes." Shankar was still thinking.

"All right, let's take some time to think things over, check the statements from the brothers and ask them to come in first thing Monday morning or if time permits we should pay them a visit. This strike is not helping."

"It would have to be Tuesday. The strike is until midnight on Monday. Although I am not on duty at the plant on Monday, we all have to be at the station to move right away to the plant if needed," Shankar said.

"Ah yes." Alok sighed. Shankar could sense that his boss wanted to get this over with as soon as possible.

"If you don't mind, sir, I do want to visit the boy's house and see his room."

"Yes. That's a good idea. Let's do that on Sunday before heading over to the plant. Give the boy's dad some room and time to grieve. Although I doubt with this sort of loss, grief lessens in any way with the passage of time." There were times when Shankar was impressed by his boss. *Maybe there's more to him than what people say about him*, he thought.

"Do you want to come with me, sir?"

"Yes."

"Come pick me up on Sunday morning around ten, and we will head over to Mr. Lal's house and take a look at the boy's room."

"Sure, sir."

"I will meet you back at the station once you are done attending the ceremony. Please offer my condolences to the professor. Sad business, this."

"Yes sir."

Shankar and Malkhan dropped Alok off at the police station and headed to the cremation.

4

The Journalist

A young man's cremation is always a sad affair. This one was even more tragic. Everyone knew that his life had been abruptly and violently ended well before his time. As he reached the grounds, Shankar could see several cars in the parking lot. It seemed a lot of Karan's friends and teachers from school had showed up to pay their last respects. Looking at the array of Fiats and Ambassadors in the parking lot gave him an idea.

"Malkhan."

"Yes, sir?"

"I have a job for you."

"Certainly, sir." Malkhan was only too eager to please. He wanted to show that he could take on more than just chauffeuring and the secretarial duties allocated to aides.

"I want you to park the car and then start looking at all the cars in the parking lot. If you find one that has a scratch in the front, either blue in color or something that seems recent, take down the license number."

"Like the blue in the garage gate at the auto shop."

"Yes." Shankar was impressed that he'd remembered. He added, "I don't want you draw any attention. Just take down their license plate numbers."

"Will do, sir," Malkhan said excitedly. He was happy that Shankar had faith in him doing more than his daily monotonous duties.

Once they had parked, Shankar got out and started slowly walking toward where the rest of the crowd had gathered. He could see the boy's father with other old gentlemen. They must be either the professor's friends or teachers from school, he figured. The Bhaskar brothers were there, too. So were all the employees from the shop. On the other side, several of his friends gathered with stoic expressions. Some of them were crying. Farther back, there were more people. Most likely, they were families of his friends and teachers from school. He could also see Nitya standing with them. She had seen him approach and had nodded gently. He went over and stood next to her, and they both waited silently till the hour-long solemn ceremony ended. Slowly, they all stood in line and filed past the professor, offering their condolences. Shankar looked at the professor, who understandably looked in pain, offered condolences on behalf of the police department, and moved on.

Nitya came up beside him while he was walking back to the parking lot. He could see that she was affected by the ceremony as well. With a calm voice, she turned to Shankar. "I hope we find who did this and bring them to justice."

Shankar nodded in agreement.

"Nitya-ji, do you have a car?"

She shook her head.

"I am heading back to the police station and can drop you at home."

"Sure."

As soon as they reached the car, Shankar told Malkhan that they would be dropping Nitya off. Malkhan knew where she lived. *Typical of a small town, I guess*, thought Shankar. Before getting in, Malkhan handed over a slip of paper with numbers on it.

Shankar smiled and whispered to Malkhan, "Not a word in the car." Malkhan nodded.

Nitya had noticed the exchange but couldn't make much of it. Once they reached the Chaturvedi residence, they all got out. Shankar graciously opened the car door and waited till she got to the entrance of her residence. Malkhan and Shankar could see that there was a woman peeking at them through the curtains of the large window. As soon as she realized that they had seen her, she quickly drew the curtains.

"Mrs. Chaturvedi, sir," Malkhan whispered, pointing to the curtains.

"Ah," replied Shankar with a smile.

He waved at Nitya. Once she was inside, he got back into the car and gave a big smile.

"Malkhan, I am impressed with you. Tell me what you saw."

Malkhan went to great lengths in describing how he had gone into stealth mode and examined every car in the parking lot. There were around thirty of them. Only two of them had scratches near the front, and one of them had a tinge of blue flakes on it. He'd taken down the license plate numbers of both cars.

"Good show, Malkhan. Now we need to check the vehicle registration files to see who they belong to."

"No need, sir. I have been a driver in Callipur for over a decade now, and I know most of the cars and drivers by their names and faces. One of them is a private taxi. It's from out of town. The other one belongs to Hari Yadav."

This name was familiar. When Shankar had first arrived in Callipur, Hari Yadav had thrown a welcome party for all the new police recruits. He was the president of the local chapter of the ruling party in the state. He was an influential politician, and the police department liked him for his tough stance on crime. As all of this was going through his mind, they arrived at the police station.

It was nearly 7:00 p.m., and it had been a very long day. He was exhausted. He headed to his office and saw a note at his desk. It was from Alok. He wrote that he was heading to the club and Shankar could meet him there.

Shankar was in no mood. He wanted to catch up on his sleep. He quickly called the club and told the manager to inform Alok that he would see him in the morning.

There was another big brown envelope on his desk. He opened it, finding all the photographs from the crime scene. He quickly glanced at them to make sure everything was there but couldn't stop yawning. He put the pictures back in the envelope and then his filing cabinet, locked everything up, and asked Malkhan to take him home. Then he changed, freshened up, ate something quickly, and settled into his bed with a new book he had picked up at the club library. There was no chance for the book to make any sort of impression on him, though. Halfway through the first page, he fell into a deep, peaceful sleep.

On the other side of town, at the Chaturvedi residence, things were anything but peaceful. Nitya was having a row with her mom about when she would marry Raj. Usually, these were monthly arguments, but since Nitya's twenty-sixth birthday, they had become almost weekly affairs. Normally, these mother-daughter love-hate fests would last a few minutes with lots of screaming, shouting, and meaningless insults followed by an uncomfortable silence and then a return to a sense of normalcy. Mr. Chaturvedi and Nitya's younger sister, Kavita, stayed out of these battles by either leaving the room or the house.

What triggered the latest row was a conversation that Mrs. Chaturvedi had with one of her childhood friends in Agra, where she learned that her friend's daughter—who was younger than Nitya—was getting married next month. That, coupled with Nitya's continued lack of seriousness about her plans with Raj, caused Mrs. Chaturvedi to go over the top. Not that she needed anything else to spice things up, but then she saw Nitya getting dropped off by someone who was not Raj. These three things were enough to bring out all of Mrs. Chaturvedi's fierceness in admonishing her daughter. Just one of these reasons would have been enough, but three on the same day seemed to her like a thunderstorm followed by an earthquake.

Mr. Chaturvedi had sensed what was going to happen and was smart enough to leave for the club earlier that evening to play cards with his friends. Under normal circumstances, his wife would invariably join him. But not tonight. She told him that she wanted to "talk" to Nitya. Kavita also knew what to expect when her sister came home. She had seen her mother peeking through the curtains and had quickly gone upstairs to her room to check out who it was. As Kavita saw Shankar wave at Nitya, she wanted desperately to warn her sister before she entered the house. But it was too late.

She could see that Nitya was tired. She tried to intervene and ask her mom to leave things until the next day. But that irritated Mrs. Chaturvedi even more, and she yelled at her to go to her room while she dealt with Nitya.

These conversations were mostly the same. They usually started with Mrs. Chaturvedi telling Nitya that she had spoken to Raj's mom. They wanted to start planning for the wedding, but they were not getting a firm date from either Nitya or Raj. This usually escalated to some pointed insults, some screaming, and a period of silence. That was it. Somewhere in there, Mrs. Chaturvedi would try to make Nitya feel guilty for giving her so much stress. She had the ability to make herself feel sad to the point of shedding tears on demand. But it seemed different this time around.

"You know, I was talking to Mrs. Saxena in Agra. Her daughter is twenty-two and is getting married next month."

"So? What does that have to do with me?"

"You are twenty-six."

"I didn't realize there was a competition."

"You know, I got married when I was twenty."

"That was in 1948, Mom. It's 1978 now. Do you think things may have changed in the last thirty years?"

"Not really!" Mrs. Chaturvedi was off and running. "Girls still need to get married at the right age."

"Unbelievable," Nitya said, raising her voice.

"And what exactly are you and Raj waiting for? You are so lucky. He is such a good boy. We have known him and his family since he was born, and you have known him since you were at school. You don't even have to go find a groom."

Nitya knew that her mom was right. She had seen the ordeal that her elder sister, Deepa, had had to go through. They had started to look for a groom when Deepa had turned twenty, and by the time she'd gotten married at twenty-two, she'd had to endure the ignominy of being paraded in front of scores of suitors, most of whom would come to the house with the mentality of either viewing a product or making a business deal. When things stalled during the first year of the search for a groom, her mom appealed to the supernatural. First, they went on a pilgrimage during their family vacation to holy sites in north and east India. When that didn't produce instant results, they started visiting holy sites in the south of the country. She then engaged matchmakers, astrologers, palmists, gurus, and yogis. At some point, the rest of the family was convinced that Mrs. Chaturvedi would bring in snake charmers if that helped.

Thankfully, their aunt, Mrs. Chaturvedi's sister, found Deepa a suitable match through a family acquaintance. Deepa had now settled in Bangalore and had a son. Nitya did not want to go through the same painful, embarrassing, and stressful ordeal. Perhaps that was one of the reasons that she was happy that Raj was there. Although they had never spoken about getting married, they were good friends who had known each other for a long time. Whenever the question of their marriage came up, they had never said no to their parents or anyone else. It seemed almost inevitable that they would end up together at some point. But now, things were not moving fast enough for Mrs. Chaturvedi.

"We have been busy in our jobs. We haven't had time to discuss this yet."

"What is there to discuss, Nitya? Just tell us a date. That's all you have to do."

"He is trying to land a promotion. I have been assigned some new projects, too. We will eventually get to it, Mom."

"And who is this fellow dropping you at home? Is that the new police officer? I have seen him at the club. He is not married. You shouldn't be going around with him. What would people think if they saw you together? I don't think Raj's parents would approve. Or even Raj." Mrs. Chaturvedi rambled on.

"I don't care what anyone thinks, Mom. He is investigating the same case that I have been assigned. And if you really want to know, he was just dropping me off. It has been a long day at work, and I have to write about this over the weekend."

"Enough with this writing stuff of yours. You need to focus on settling down. I hope this nonsense with *The Callipur Post* gets over soon. I wonder how you will ever have a family if you keep working these long hours. It's fine for now, but it will not work once you get married, I am sure." This time, Mrs. Chaturvedi had hit a nerve.

"Mom, I want to keep working. I worked hard to be a journalist. What I do is not nonsense, at least not to me. I have made a name for myself. I have an identity of my own. I want my own career. You know, it's funny that Raj or his parents have never brought up my job or career. Every time it comes up, they have been fine with it, and Raj has been supportive. It seems you are the one who has a problem. Are you sure you were married in 1948 and not some other century?"

At this point, Nitya was screaming at the top her voice. Her eyes were filled with tears.

Mrs. Chaturvedi realized that she had crossed a line. Part of her wanted to. Nitya knew that, too. She knew what would irk her daughter and could be hurtful when she wanted to be. Then she calmed down with some sense of remorse in her voice, looked at Nitya, and put her arm around her shoulders.

"I have to worry. I am your mom. Then we will have to think about Kavita, too."

"Mom, Kavita is eighteen. Take it easy."

"All I am saying is that our families have been friends for years. You and Raj are a good match. I have never heard you say otherwise. No one else seems to be worried except for me and Raj's mom. Look at your dad. He hardly spends any time talking to me nowadays. He is always busy at the club."

I wonder why that is, Nitya thought but decided to call a truce.

"OK, Mom. I promise that Raj and I will talk, and we will let you know. But please, let's not have this conversation each time someone else's kid is tying the knot."

"OK, I won't." Both Nitya and Mrs. Chaturvedi knew that that was a complete lie. But they were both exhausted and decided to end this round here.

"Have you eaten anything?"

"I am tired, Mom. Can I please have my dinner in my room?"

"Sure."

Nitya went to her room, where Kavita was waiting for her. She had obviously heard everything. It was nothing new. Although Nitya was closer to her older sister Deepa in age, in everything else, she was similar to Kavita. She also knew that Kavita looked up to her. There were lots of reasons for that. In a country where most people wanted to get a government job with a pension or become a doctor, a lawyer, or an engineer, Nitya had charted her own path. She knew that she had a knack for writing. She did well at school, well enough to get into a journalism program in Pune, and convinced her parents to let her study there. Once she had finished, she had landed a job with *The Callipur Post* on her own merit and initiative. *The Callipur Post* was not a national daily, but it was one of the most coveted regional newspapers with a wide circulation. In the five years that she had worked there, she had made a name for herself as a good investigative journalist and writer and had received a statewide award. For anyone to have done all that would be commendable, even more so for a woman. She had to overcome the crude remarks, backhanded compliments, chauvinism, and unwanted advances from some of her male peers and bosses. India had moved forward quite a bit in the sphere of women's rights since the late 1940s after independence, but not fast enough for Nitya.

She was happy to see Kavita. They talked while she changed, ate, and got ready for bed.

"What's going on with you and Raj?" Kavita asked.

"Don't you start now."

"You know, Mom was right about one thing. You should make up your mind one way or the other."

"I just don't want to end up as a housewife like Deepa. I like what I do, and I don't know how things are with Raj. We spend time without talking much. Lately, I don't feel that I need to share stuff with him. I still like him, and part of me wants to be with him. But I am scared to let go of him, too."

"Well," Kavita continued, easing into her sister's bed for a hug, "if it were up to me, I would just run away with someone like Shankar and not worry about anything else."

Nitya started laughing. "So, you know who Shankar is?"

"Yes. I have seen him at the club a couple of times with my friends. He is always in the library. He never comes to talk to us." Kavita sighed.

"Oh, the horror. Someone who actually likes books more than Bollywood. So, what do you know about him?"

"Nothing except that he is single and good-looking."

They both started laughing. They talked a bit more. She gave her younger sister a hug and ordered her out of her room.

As Nitya hit the pillow after a long, exhausting day, she started thinking about the letter that she had received from one of the national newspapers in India. They had written to her complimenting her on the award that she had received. They had also asked whether she would consider taking a job with them and moving to a big city like Bombay or Delhi. Working at *The Callipur Post* had its pros and cons. It was a good job, and she was in her comfort zone. Because it was a small newspaper, she had no other supervisors than the editor. For the most part, she was free to do her own work in her own time. The management was happy because she was good, and she delivered. But there was a downside, too. She had spent five years there. There really wasn't any scope for promotion or growth. She would have to move out and away from Callipur if she wanted to advance or take on more exciting roles and assignments. At some point, she did want to move to a national daily. Most of their offices and jobs were in the big cities. She hadn't mentioned the letter or its contents to anyone. She could only imagine the effect it would have on her mom. She wondered why she wasn't comfortable discussing it with Raj, either.

Then she started thinking about the case. What had Malkhan written on that paper that he had handed to Shankar in the parking lot? She had to find out. Then she fell asleep.

5

The Lawyer

Almost the entire police department was tied up manning barricades at the steel plant on Saturday. Alok and all the other officers were ordered to be at the plant at 6:30 in the morning and some makeshift camps had been constructed for taking short breaks. The labor union had called for a three-day strike and although the management and union leaders were negotiating, things were not moving fast enough for either party. Thankfully, the protests outside the plant were largely peaceful. Apart from a few verbal insults hurled at the police, the protesters seemed content in making lots of noise and listening to speeches from their leaders outside the gates. Both Shankar and Alok were frustrated that they could not continue their investigation into Karan's death and the entire day was lost at the plant. Shankar sometimes wondered and questioned on how things were prioritized by his bosses.

Maintaining calm at the plant during the strike was important, but at the same time, there was a killer on the loose. He also knew that the department did not have much of a choice. The elected officials were very sensitive to labor unrests and did not want a repeat of what happened last time. All other investigations took a back seat. He couldn't help but wonder if the gang of robbers knew this as well and whether they would take advantage of the fact that most of the police force were stationed at one location. The protesters started dispersing around 9:00 p.m. By midnight everyone had left, and Shankar was told that he could leave the site. He went home and he was happy that he wasn't scheduled to go back to the plant until Monday.

Shankar had asked Malkhan to pick him up at his residence on Sunday morning. They wanted to pay a visit to Karan Lal's house to see if there was something in his room or belongings that could help them with their investigation. Shankar arrived at the Vij residence at ten a.m. and was greeted by a servant, who led him to the living room. Once he was seated, Mrs. Vij entered.

Mrs. Sonali Vij came from a different India, an India largely unaffected by whatever else might be happening in the country. She came from a rich, affluent family and made sure that everyone knew that she belonged to the entitled class. People like her seemed to do well regardless of whether the country was going through a recession, recovering from a disaster, or dealing with a different party in power. They had the money and power to both influence and adapt. She had been married to Alok for ten years, ever since he'd graduated from the academy, and both of their families made sure they wielded whatever influence was necessary to ensure that Alok fulfilled his ambition of reaching the top of the police service. Alok hadn't disappointed, of course. He had fared better than all his peers, and he and his wife knew that their stint in Callipur was temporary before Alok would be transferred to Delhi.

She was well known at the club. She also considered herself a bit of a misfit in Callipur. From her perspective, it was a tiny town with small people dealing with smaller problems. But she didn't harp on that much. Both her parents and in-laws had assured her that Alok's transfer order and promotion to Delhi was imminent.

There was one other reason why they had to move that no one wanted to discuss. Ten years of marriage had not produced any children. A move to Delhi would help in getting the right medical advice and treatment for that to happen.

On this Sunday, Mrs. Vij was upset that Alok had to go off to work instead of taking her to a luncheon. She knew Shankar from the club.

"Good morning, Shankar. How are you?"

"I am doing well, madam."

"Tea, coffee, anything?"

"I am fine, madam."

Just as she was going to ask him about the case, Alok walked in.

"Hi, Shankar."

"Good morning, sir."

"Ready, are we?"

"Yes."

Alok mumbled something to his wife as he walked out. She smiled and went back inside the house. On the way to the Lal residence, Alok told Shankar that they might have a breakthrough in the robbery case. He also told him that Maheshwar Mishra had asked for a meeting on Friday specifically about the Karan Lal case.

As they reached the house, they saw the professor sitting outside surrounded by some other people. The house was in a state of mourning. Even though it was sunny and bright, one look at the house made Alok and Shankar sad.

"Let's make this quick, Shankar, and be delicate while asking any questions."

"Yes, sir," Shankar agreed.

Once they were inside the house, the rest of the people moved to one corner of the big living room. Both Alok and Shankar offered their condolences to the professor.

"He was a good boy, you know. Initially, I didn't want him to work at the garage. But he insisted, and I caved. He enjoyed working there and was happy," said Mr. Lal, holding back tears.

"Mr. Lal, we do have to ask you a few questions. If this is not a good time, we will be happy to come back later," said Alok thoughtfully.

"No. Let's do this now and get it over with."

"When was the last time you saw Karan?"

"Thursday morning when he left for work."

"What time was that?"

"Around nine thirty a.m."

"Was he in good spirits, sir? Did he seem worried?" inquired Shankar.

"No. As I said, he was happy at his job."

"Were you not worried when he didn't come home?"

"No. I have a heart condition, and I take a lot of medication that puts me to sleep. I went to bed around eight thirty p.m. Usually, Shankar is back between ten and ten thirty p.m. He eats something and goes to bed. Our conversations are usually in the morning."

"We understand that the garage closes at eight p.m., and it's not too far from the house. Any reason why he gets home so late?"

"He is . . . was a young man. He usually goes to the Roop tea stall across from the garage after work to meet his friends before coming home."

Shankar noted it down.

"Do you know if he had plans to meet anyone?"

"No. But he didn't usually tell me. He was a good boy. No vices, if that's what you are asking."

Broken Dreams: A Callipur Murder Mystery

"Mr. Lal, is there anyone else who lives in this house that was with you that evening?" Alok asked.

"Karan's mother died when he was very young. So it's just the two of us. We have part-time help who comes to clean the house and cook in the afternoon. But she had left around six p.m."

"Is there anyone that you can think of that may have done this?" Alok asked.

Mr. Lal started crying, and they weren't sure if he heard the question. It was time for them to leave. Alok turned to Shankar to see if he wanted to ask any other questions.

"We have one last request, sir. Can we please see Karan's room? If you can just point it out to us, we will take a look ourselves."

"Sure," Mr. Lal said, regaining some of his composure.

He waved at someone in the group, and an old gentleman stepped forward.

"Manohar, can you please take these gentlemen and show them to Karan's room?" He then turned to Alok and Shankar and said, "I hope you find who did this."

"We will, and thank you, sir," Alok replied, and Saumya Lal slowly walked out of the room.

Karan's room looked like he had a passion for cars and movies. There were posters on every inch of the walls. Half of them were of cars, and half of them were movie posters with cars in them. The room had a small bed, a desk with a table lamp, and a chair. There was a bookshelf with books mostly about cars, fiction, and sports. Near the window there were some school pictures. He appeared to be active in sports with all sorts of team photos from his previous schools. The rest of the room had nothing much to offer by way of clues.

"Oh," Alok said, looking at one of the photographs. "That's Manoj." He turned and showed Shankar the picture. "That's Hari Yadav's son."

Shankar recognized him as well. He had seen him at the cremation. Shankar still hadn't told Alok about the whole business with the cars and license plates. He wanted to wait till they were back at the station. Shankar looked at the picture and handed it back to Alok. The cupboards contained more of the same: clothes, pictures, some papers, certificates. A basket in the corner had some greasy overalls from the auto shop. Shankar looked under the bed and found a box with some more pictures. Some of them showed Karan when he was young and in a different school. There was also a picture of him and his mother.

There was also an old camera with film still inside. He was into photography, based on the photos taken around Callipur. People, places, things, and of course, cars.

Shankar wondered what the film had on it. He turned to Alok and said, "I am going to ask Mr. Lal if he will allow us to develop this film. We will share the pictures with him, of course."

"Sure. I think we are done here."

"Yes," Shankar replied.

They left the room and thanked Mr. Lal one more time. He gave Shankar his permission to develop the pictures in the camera.

"Please do return the camera and the photos to me as soon as you are done."

"Absolutely, sir. Thank you."

On the way back, they stopped by a print shop. Shankar told the owner that he wanted the photos processed and the camera returned within a day.

Once they were back at the police station, Shankar proceeded to inform Alok about the scratches on Hari Yadav's car and the taxi, along with the matching paint from the garage gates. Alok's expression immediately became serious and pensive.

"Let's think this through, Shankar. There's nothing to suggest that the scratch had been made the same night. Unless there are any witnesses, we can't really do much. And let's remember, we are talking about Hari Yadav here. You know who he is."

"Yes, sir." Shankar knew it didn't amount to much on its own.

But he pressed on. "Sir, Manoj Yadav and Karan Lal knew each other, based on all the pictures. At the very least, can we ask Mr. Yadav and his son their whereabouts during the time of death?"

"Based on what?" Alok was visibly annoyed. "We can't just go asking people things like this based on a past photo and scratch on a car. At this point, both are completely unrelated."

"Right, sir." Shankar knew Alok was right and didn't want to irritate him any further.

"What we can do," Alok said, "is go to his school and find out if they know of anything that might help us. The problem is that his class has already graduated, and his friends are in different colleges. But maybe you can talk to some of his teachers."

"I will get to it on Tuesday once we are done with the strike at the plant."

"Yes. This wretched strike is not helping things, is it, Shankar?"

"No, sir." Shankar again sensed Alok's restlessness to solve the case.

"I am off, then," Alok said. "I will be at the steel plant all day tomorrow. I know you are on duty there as well. I am not sure we will be able to do much on this. Let's catch up on Tuesday when the Bhaskar brothers come in for their interviews and detailed statements. I want you to go over their preliminary statements and be prepared to ask questions that might shed some light on all of this. And oh, by the way, I forgot to tell you. They will have a lawyer with them, Harsh. I am not sure if you have met him at the club."

"I must have seen him, sir. Probably know him by face."

"Yes. He is sharp and thorough. I think you will like him." Alok waved and left.

Shankar was curious as to why the Bhaskars had employed a lawyer. Both Praveen and Pramod Bhaskar were at the auto shop during various times on the night of the slaying. But there was nothing to indicate that they were responsible. Both seemed to be frail old men who didn't have the physical strength to strike the fatal blow. So, why the lawyer? Who was this lawyer? He would find out soon enough.

Before he could set his mind to the Bhaskars, Shankar wanted to follow up on the two cars with the scratches. His first stop was to inquire about the taxi. He went to the taxi stand, spoke to the owner, and asked him to check the records of the car in question with the license plate number Malkhan had noted. It was a dead end. As per his records, that car was not in Callipur that night and had returned in the morning. It had been rented out to an out-of-town official visiting the port and was parked in the port guesthouse all night. The driver confirmed that that was the case. He had returned to Callipur only the following morning. The scratches, the driver said, had been there for at least the last six weeks. All he could say was that the car was in a parking lot near the movie theater, and when he had come back after a short tea break at a nearby stall, he had noticed the scratches.

Then there was Hari Yadav's car. Shankar had checked the list of cars serviced in the garage. Both cars were not on the list of ever getting repaired or serviced there in the last eight weeks. He remembered the conversation with Alok and decided to see if anyone in the vicinity of the garage had seen the vehicle on the night in question. He would have to be discreet without arousing any suspicion that he was trying to link it to the case. The only place that he could think of near the garage where people might have seen the car would be the Roop tea stall across from the gates to the entrance of the auto shop. It was a long shot. But he decided to go there and see what he could find.

He went home, released Malkhan and the police Jeep, and decided to change into civilian clothes and walk to the tea stall. It was a good thirty-minute walk from his apartment. Along the way, he tried to think how he could establish the whereabouts of Hari Yadav and his family without actually asking them.

Once he reached the tea stall, he found that it was quite full. It was just a big covered shed with some stools and benches inside and outside for folks to sit. Its clientele was varied. During the week, there were workers from the auto shop, the garage's clients waiting for their cars to be serviced, students who could not afford fancy restaurants, and folks from the nearby courthouse and movie theater. It was well located, clean, and convenient. On this Sunday, the courts and garage were closed, but there were still people from the movie theater and some students with bicycles who had stopped by to spend time with their friends.

As Shankar walked in, he spotted Roop Madan, the owner of the establishment. He was at the makeshift counter barking orders and instructions to clean up. As Shankar walked past the tables to talk to him, he heard an unfamiliar voice call out to him.

"Mr. Shankar Sen?" Shankar turned around to see a gentleman with a briefcase, which was odd for a Sunday.

"Yes."

"My name is Harsh Thakur. I am the lawyer representing the Bhaskar brothers." Shankar recognized him from the club. He had seen him a few times, occasionally talking to Nitya. But they'd never spoken. He had heard that Harsh was good lawyer. Then there was some gossip about his ex-wife that he chose not to bother with. Perhaps he should have paid more attention.

"Ah yes, so I heard," Shankar replied.

"Yes, I spoke to Alok earlier today to inform him that I will be coming with my clients on Tuesday."

"Right," Shankar said, wondering what he was doing here on a Sunday with a briefcase in his hand when the garage and the courts were closed.

"Well, I must be leaving now. It was nice seeing you here. We will meet again on Tuesday."

They shook hands, and after Harsh left, Shankar went up to Roop Madan, introduced himself, and asked to speak to him privately. Once they found themselves in a corner of the shed with no one nearby, Shankar asked him whether he kept track of cars coming in and out of the garage.

"We see a lot of cars coming in and out. But we really don't keep track."

"What about the night Karan Lal was killed?"

"Yes. There were a few cars, but at night, it's hard to see who is coming in and out. But I did notice Pramod Bhaskar coming by at around nine p.m. in his car. What struck me as odd was that he was driving and not the driver. We had just started closing up. Then he left after fifteen or twenty minutes. After that, I can't say. We heard about Karan's death in the morning. Really sad. Karan was a good kid and used to often come here with his friends after work."

Shankar thought for a minute.

"When Pramod was leaving, was he alone, or was there someone else in the car?"

"Well, that's the other odd bit. When he left, it seemed that there was someone in the back seat who had leaned over towards the window on the far side. It was dark, and I couldn't see who it was."

"One last question. I see that you can see the gates of the shop from here. Was there ever any accident that you saw? Maybe a car hitting or scraping the gates?"

"Yes. But that was many weeks ago. I remember Praveen Bhaskar coming in that evening for his tea in a really bad mood, complaining that some kids were learning how to drive. One had scraped the gates."

"Did he say who the kid was?"

"Yes. I remember because it was one of Karan's friends. Manoj Yadav."

"Thank you. You have been of great help."

"It's funny. You are the second person asking me all these questions today."

"Let me guess," Shankar replied. "The gentleman who just left with the briefcase was the first one?"

"Yes. He is a lawyer."

As Shankar started walking back home, he started replaying everything that Roop Madan had told him in his head. He was right that Hari Yadav's son, Manoj Yadav, had grazed the garage gates while driving, but it had happened a few weeks ago and had nothing to do with what happened the night Karan was killed. The more interesting bit, of course, was that Pramod Bhaskar had come to the garage at around 9:00 p.m. and then left twenty minutes later with someone in the back seat. And then there was the lawyer, Harsh, who had been there before him and had all the same answers.

Meanwhile, Harsh Thakur was back in his office, meticulously making notes and preparing statements on behalf of his clients, the Bhaskar brothers. He had known Praveen Bhaskar for a long time. He had represented him in earlier cases. The first one was involving a land dispute as the garage was expanding. Then a few years ago, there was another case brought against the garage by a client for wrecking his car during some bodywork. And then there was the incident with the robbery. When the gang of robbers had hit the garage, they had stolen car parts and tools and had broken some furniture while ransacking the place, looking for money. Praveen Bhaskar had called Harsh to deal with the insurance claim.

Harsh did not know Pramod Bhaskar that well. The younger brother had only moved to Callipur a couple of years ago. When Pramod had called frantically the night Karan was killed after the police had left, Harsh knew that something was wrong. He agreed to represent them and had started gathering relevant details right away. He had already interviewed all the employees, obtained records of Praveen's visit to the hospital that night, and spoken to Roop Madan. It had been a busy day. He knew that in the Tuesday meeting with the police, furnishing an accurate timeline for the brothers' activities was key in proving their innocence.

As lawyers go, Harsh Thakur was a bit of an oddity. He didn't really want to be a lawyer. He was from Barrackpore, which was a few hours away from Callipur. In college, he had been pursuing a degree in psychology when he fell in love with Rohini Seth, a girl from Bombay who was a law student at the neighboring college. After dating for a few months, she managed to convince Harsh to switch to the law program. Programs in the university were not so flexible that he could easily switch. He ended up losing a year, but he prepared for the exams and scraped through.

Broken Dreams: A Callipur Murder Mystery

Rohini and Harsh were an item throughout their college years. Everyone who knew them knew that they were meant for each other. Everyone, that is, except their parents. Rohini's parents were industrialists and wanted her to marry someone that would grow the family business. Harsh's parents, on the other hand, were landlords in Barrackpore and came from a very conservative family. They wanted Harsh to marry someone in their same caste and had already selected a bride for him. When Rohini and Harsh decided to elope, both families saw the marriage as a betrayal. The couple moved to Callipur because there weren't too many lawyers in the area, and the town was expanding with industries and people moving in from the rest of the country.

Things changed when Akash was born. Both sets of parents mellowed somewhat, but it was Rohini's parents on whom their grandson's birth had the biggest impact. Rohini's father needed a boy to whom to entrust the business. Her family hatched up a plan to get Rohini to move back to Bombay. They invited her over and lavished her with gifts and comfort that Harsh and Rohini simply couldn't afford or get in a small town like Callipur.

When she returned to Callipur, her mother came back with her. Within a few weeks, she had created enough friction between Harsh and Rohini to make them grow apart. She had also managed to convince her daughter of the better schooling in Bombay for Akash and the opportunities that a big city could provide. Harsh's long hours at work trying to establish a growing practice and his constant travel hadn't helped. Finally, Rohini decided to leave, and the love affair for the ages came to an end.

It took a couple of years for the divorce to be finalized. Once that was done, her parents had her paired off with another divorcé, Sunil, from a business family. Their families had a ready explanation of why Rohini's and Sunil's first marriages had failed. They were immature kids who didn't get their parents' blessing, so obviously, they were destined to fail. Their second stint was an arranged affair because they had learned from their past mistakes. Their parents had most graciously selected, reviewed, and blessed their new partners, so obviously, this union would last forever. What could possibly go wrong?

The one thing that Rohini had insisted on and that Harsh was grateful for was that Akash spend time with his father. Each summer and during Diwali, Akash visited his father in Callipur.

While Rohini had moved on, Harsh was still single. Divorce was frowned upon in big cities, and in a small town like Callipur, it was borderline sinful. Harsh nevertheless had managed to establish a decent practice, and the people in town had warmed up to him because of his friendly, helpful nature. In the club, most of the ladies would still refer to him as "the divorced one" while talking among themselves, but there were others who simply didn't care. Harsh, for the most part, had learned to ignore the bad vibes and was reasonably happy with his life. He missed Akash and often thought of moving to Bombay to be close to him. Akash had asked him about that and had also told him that his mother would approve.

All of that was far from his mind at the moment. He finished his notes and draft statements for Tuesday and decided to look them over one more time. He then called the Bhaskars and told them that he would be coming over to review their statements with them first thing on Monday. The Bhaskar brothers were both happy and relieved that Harsh was representing them.

As Harsh turned in for the night, he wondered what Shankar knew about the case and what surprises lay in store. He had seen Shankar at the club. He was a quiet one. That's what worried him. He also knew that Maheshwar Mishra liked him. Mishra-ji didn't like everyone in the police department, only the good ones.

6

The Robbery

When Shankar arrived at the police station early on Monday, the only conversation in the corridors was regarding the robbery case. Several members of the task force were still in town. It seemed that an arrest was imminent. From what he had heard from Alok, the gang was spread out across different towns, and the police were trying to coordinate some sort of joint raid. But it was not his case. He was surprised to see Alok there, and not at the plant. One of the other officers told him that things at the plant were calm and not everyone would be needed on site. But they had to be in the office and be ready to move quickly if needed.

He went to his office and found a brown envelope from the photo store waiting for him. It had the pictures from the undeveloped film in Karan's camera. Malkhan had neatly placed all the statements from the workers and other case-related documents on his desk. It was time to do his homework.

He started with all the statements from the shop employees. They seemed to be in order. He would have to check the alibis this week to make sure that no one was in the garage at the time of the incident. Then he read the preliminary statements from the brothers. They seemed vague and there were holes in the timelines. He wasn't happy about that. If not for the strike, he would have summoned them to the station or headed over to question them right away. He knew he couldn't. He also knew that they were expected at the station the following morning and he could question them at that time. He called the lab in the state capital processing the fingerprints from the room in the shop upstairs. No surprises there. The Bhaskar brothers and the shop employees had voluntarily given police their prints, and the prints from the room all belonged to the Bhaskar brothers. He looked at the photographs from the crime scene in case he had missed anything. Then there was the postmortem report. He went through inventory list that one of the workers had provided about the shop's tools. Some tools were missing, but the register had not been updated, so there really wasn't much to deduce from it.

Finally, he got to the latest set of pictures from Karan's camera. They were all of people and places around town. There were a few pictures of the garage workers and another one of his friends from school during graduation. Shankar recognized some of the faces from the cremation ceremony and from the photos in the box he had seen under Karan's bed.

One photo was not very clear. It was a picture of the back of a car with two people in the back seat. It was a rather intimate photograph, a couple embracing and about to kiss. He recognized Pramod Bhaskar from the garage, but he was sure that the woman was not Pramod's wife. He had seen pictures of the Bhaskar family in the offices of each of the brothers. This woman was not in them. So, why did Karan take this picture? And who was the woman? He couldn't recall whether he had seen her in the club. But from what he could make out, it appeared that the photograph had been taken in the parking lot of the club.

He called for Malkhan. He showed him the picture and asked him who the woman was.

"That's Mrs. Mathur. Mr. Swaroop Mathur's wife, Rita Mathur."

"Are you sure?"

"You must have seen her in the club."

Broken Dreams: A Callipur Murder Mystery

Maybe I should go to this club more often. It seems all these characters are there all the time, Shankar thought. Well, the one person who would know for sure was Alok. He decided to wait till Alok was free to ask him. In the meantime, he decided to start writing his report, drawing a timeline of everything they knew so far.

Finally, Alok walked into Shankar's office. He was in a good mood. The robbery case had made a lot of headway, and it would be solved within a week.

"That's great news, sir."

"Yes. Maybe this whole business will be sorted out as well once we get those scums. By the way, the strike at the plant seems peaceful. But we may need to go there later today."

"Yes, sir."

Shankar picked up the photograph and handed it to Alok.

"This is one of the pictures from Karan Lal's camera."

Alok looked at it carefully and said, "That's the younger Bhaskar brother with Rita Mathur. I have seen her at the club."

"It was in his camera," Shankar said.

"Spicy stuff. Not sure how this relates to the case, though."

"I haven't figured that out yet. But we may need to ask Mrs. Mathur as well."

"What? Based on this picture? Perhaps, yes. Well, let's see what the Bhaskars say tomorrow, and then we will take it from there," Alok said.

Shankar knew he was probably right.

"They are coming here at ten with their lawyer."

"Yes. Harsh is a good lawyer. I'll bet he has already prepared a timeline and statements. He is very thorough."

"One more thing, sir. It's about Hari Yadav's son, Manoj. It seems that he was learning how to drive and grazed the garage gates with his car. But that happened a few weeks ago. The folks in the tea stall across the garage confirmed that."

Alok sighed when he heard this. He handed the photograph back to Shankar and said with a firm but calm voice, "You need to drop this. We know Karan and Manoj went to the same school. But he is not the only one. Unless you can place Manoj at the garage at the same time as the murder, you have to move on."

Once again, Shankar knew that Alok was right. But he wanted to find out where Manoj Yadav was on the night of the incident. He would just have to do it without letting his boss know or directly asking the Yadavs.

As Shankar thought about all of this, Alok got up and said, "Unless there's anything else, I need to get back to the other meetings. You know, the robbery stuff. We will talk tomorrow when the Bhaskars get here."

"Yes, sir."

Once Alok left the room, Shankar went back to his report and timeline from the night of the incident. He also made a mental note to visit Karan's school during the week to see if he could find anything else to go on. Just as he was about to start making some phone calls to check the alibis of the shop employees, Shankar along with Alok and some other officers were summoned to the steel plant. Once they got there, they saw a large crowd gathered just outside the main gate. There was some pushing and shoving for a brief period. One of the constables got slightly injured while falling, but the rest of the day was largely uneventful, and they all heaved a sigh of relief once the strike ended at midnight.

On Tuesday, Harsh and the Bhaskar brothers arrived and were waiting in the police station before Shankar and Alok showed up. From the initial exchange, it was evident that Alok and Harsh knew each other rather well from the club. Harsh informed the officers that he was representing both brothers. Shankar had booked an interview room for the visit and told Harsh to bring them in one at a time.

They started with Praveen Bhaskar. His statement was straightforward. He was in the garage and had started drinking in the room upstairs around 7:30 p.m. He was not aware of who was on the shop floor or when he passed out. The next thing he remembered was his brother trying to wake him up by throwing cold water on his face. He remembered struggling to get down the stairs and then into his brother's car. After that, he only remembered waking up in the middle of the night in the hospital. The records at the hospital verified that his brother brought him in around 9:45 p.m. He had come to his senses in the middle of the night and spent the whole night at the hospital before being discharged the next day. Praveen wasn't in the garage when Karan died between 11:00 p.m. and midnight. Alok and Shankar asked a few more questions about whether there had been trouble between the other employees and Karan. Praveen backed up the statements from the workers that Karan was well liked. There seemed to be no animosity between him and the others in the shop.

Once Shankar and Alok were both satisfied, they moved on to Pramod Bhaskar.

Harsh handed over his detailed statement. The officers were impressed with how well it was written. While they read the statement, Harsh spoke.

"I know my client had said during the night of the incident that he went to the auto shop at around one a.m. and found the victim's body. That is true. But he wants to add that he was at the shop earlier at nine p.m. as well. He had gone home after going to the movies. But he found that his brother had not returned home. He went to check the garage and found him intoxicated and delirious in the room where you found wet sheets and bottles of alcohol. He took him to the hospital and got him admitted him there at nine forty-five p.m. He stayed there until he knew that his brother was feeling better. He then returned to the auto shop to clean things up before the next morning. That's when he found Karan lying on the floor. Then he called the police and the ambulance. The rest you already know and is in the statement."

Alok spoke first, addressing Harsh. "So, you are saying that at the time of the murder, your client was in the hospital?"

"Yes," Pramod replied. "I have nothing to do with what happened to Karan. Why on earth would I do anything like this to him? He was a good boy, and I liked him. Everyone liked him."

"What about when you first went to the shop at nine p.m.? Did you see Karan there?" Alok asked.

"No," Pramod replied.

It was Shankar's turn to ask the next question. "Mr. Bhaskar, why didn't you mention this before? It is not in your preliminary statement."

Harsh looked at Pramod and nodded. "It's because I didn't want anyone to know about my brother's state. He has a bad drinking habit, and it is embarrassing."

Shankar continued. "Can anyone confirm that you were at the hospital with your brother the entire time?"

"I don't know. I can't say. I mean, I did go outside for a smoke a couple of times."

Broken Dreams: A Callipur Murder Mystery

"So, it is possible that you could have come back to the auto shop and then gone back to the hospital?" Shankar said.

"Now, wait a minute," Harsh said. "My client has provided an accurate statement of his whereabouts. We came here in good faith to aid with the investigation to help find who did this to this young man. Mr. Bhaskar wasn't aware that he needed to provide alibis for all his movements to prove that he has nothing to do with all of this. And he doesn't. Unless you have something to charge him with, we are done here."

"Not quite," Shankar said. "I have a couple of more questions. Of course, it is entirely up to you whether you want to stay and answer them." He placed the picture of Pramod and Rita Mathur on the table. "We found this on Karan's camera."

"This has nothing to do with the case," Pramod replied, visibly shaken and angry.

"Is Mrs. Rita Mathur the one you went to the movies with that night?" Shankar asked. Alok was silent.

"Yes," Pramod replied in a feeble voice.

"Will she be able to corroborate that?"

"Does she really need to be dragged into this? Can we count on your discretion in not letting her family know?" Pramod pleaded.

"A young man is dead. I don't care about your affair. That's not my concern. But we do need to find out what happened that night. We will be confirming it with Mrs. Mathur. So, just to recap, you went to the movies with Mrs. Mathur that night, dropped her off, and then went home, didn't see your brother, went to the auto shop around nine p.m., saw him intoxicated, took him to the hospital, and then came back to see Karan lying on the floor at one a.m. Does that sound about right?" Shankar paused to give Pramod a chance to respond.

"Yes."

"One last question. Were you aware that Karan had found out about your affair?"

"No."

Shankar looked at Alok and was happy that Alok had let him do all the questioning. He could see Alok was satisfied. But it was Harsh that broke the silence.

"We have one more statement to provide." He handed over what looked like a medical report to Shankar.

"What's this, Harsh?" Alok asked.

"It is from Mr. Pramod Bhaskar's doctor. It's about his hands. He is currently getting treated for an incident that happened in the past that has made his arms very weak. He cannot lift heavy objects or use excessive force. In fact, he has trouble lifting his hands above his shoulders. The details are all in the report. The doctor will be happy to confirm that." Harsh then gently tapped on his client's arm, and they both got up.

"Unless there's anything else, we would like to leave."

"Thank you, Harsh and Mr. Bhaskar. If we do think of anything else, we will let you know," Alok said.

"There's one other thing," Shankar said. Both Pramod and Harsh were exasperated at this point.

"We would like the statement of your wife, Mrs. Bhaskar, the evening of the murder as well," Shankar said softly.

When they left, Alok and Shankar knew that the medical report probably exonerated Pramod. Alok asked Shankar to check it out anyway.

"Harsh is a good lawyer," Shankar said.

"Yes, and as you can see, very thorough," Alok replied and headed towards the door.

"So, what's next?"

"A visit to the school. Checking the hospital to see if anyone can confirm whether Mr. Bhaskar was there all the time that night between nine and about one. Talk to his doctor about his arm injury. Talk to Mrs. Rita Mathur, and check out the alibis of all the workers." Shankar deliberately left out telling Alok about wanting to find out about Manoj Yadav's whereabouts that night. He still had to figure out how to do that.

"I think I will leave you to it, then. For the alibis, feel free to take help from your other colleagues who questioned them in the first place. It may be faster."

"Yes, sir."

"Good work today with the questioning. I liked it."

"Thank you, sir."

Shankar engaged Arun and Sanjay, who had helped in taking down the initial reports, to start checking on the alibis of the employees from the auto shop. Shankar had already read them and knew that it wouldn't take long for them to find out if anything was amiss.

He then left for the hospital. There were several people at the hospital that had seen Pramod Bhaskar bringing in his brother and waiting for him that night. None of them could recall a prolonged period of absence. He was indeed getting treated by a specialist for an arm injury. It was unlikely, given the lack of strength in his arms, that he could have struck the blow that killed Karan.

Next stop was the Mathur residence. When he got there, Rita Mathur opened the door. She let him into a large living room. He saw that there were pictures of the family on the walls and side tables.

"Is that your son?" asked Shankar, pointing to the picture of a tall, handsome hockey player.

"Yes, that's Rajesh. Is he in trouble?" asked Mrs. Mathur with a worried look on her face.

"No, not at all. I am actually here to talk to you."

"Oh." She seemed relieved.

"As you must have read in the papers, a young boy was killed."

"You are talking about Karan."

"Yes."

"Yes, I know. Rajesh and Karan went to the same school. There was that reporter who came here earlier as well."

"Nitya?" Shankar asked, curious why she would show up here.

"Yes. We have seen her at the club a few times."

"What I want to know, Mrs. Mathur, is whether you went to the movies earlier that evening with Mr. Pramod Bhaskar," Shankar asked as gently and delicately as possible. He could see that he had made her uncomfortable.

"Yes," she replied, sounding embarrassed.

"What time did you return home?"

"A little before nine. Pramod dropped me off at the street corner, and I walked home."

"Who was at home that night?" Shankar went on.

"The rest of the family. All of them. We were thinking of going to the club but decided against it and were all home the entire night."

Broken Dreams: A Callipur Murder Mystery

"Thank you, Mrs. Mathur. You will have to make a written statement to that effect. The rest of the family, too, on their whereabouts."

"Will you tell them about me and Pramod?"

"No. All I need to know is where you all were and your alibis."

"Thank you."

Shankar headed back to the police station. When he arrived, there was almost a festive atmosphere. As soon as he entered his office, he learned that multiple arrests had been made in the robbery case with several suspects apprehended in Callipur and neighboring towns. Almost everyone had smiles on their faces, and he could see Alok, Maheshwar Mishra, and all the other officers huddled in one of the bigger rooms, congratulating one another.

As soon as Alok saw him, he waved Shankar over. Amid all the celebration, Shankar got the details. Some police informers in a neighboring town had tipped them off. The task force had two of the gang members under surveillance for a few days, and they discovered that they were planning a daring robbery at a big jewelry store in Ranipat. They laid a trap and caught them. They were also able to apprehend several accomplices and find their safe houses. Needless to say, everyone was happy that the gang had been apprehended. So was Shankar.

"Let's talk before you leave, Shankar," Alok told him.

"Sure, sir."

Shankar thought Alok probably wanted an update on his case. But once Alok came into his office, he had news for Shankar.

"I may have good news regarding the boy's case, Shankar."

"What's that, sir?"

"It seems one of the suspects in Ranipat may have mentioned that some members of his gang were in Callipur that night."

"Did he specifically say that they came to the garage and killed Karan Lal, sir?"

"No, it's all a bit muddy at the moment. When the suspect was interrogated, he confessed to multiple crimes, but we're a little short on the details as of now. I have asked my counterpart in Ranipat to get the details."

Shankar was not convinced. Interrogations that beat up suspects made them confess to almost anything. All interrogations were not beatings. But Shankar knew that the police department was under a lot of pressure to solve the robbery case. They had started resorting to heavy handed tactics in dealing with suspects while questioning and interrogating them.

"Sir, can I go to Ranipat and interview this suspect?"

"Yes, I had asked about that, but the commissioner refused the request. They want to have an airtight case in front of the magistrate and are not allowing anyone not directly involved with the investigation to handle any of the suspects," Alok said and sighed.

"But sir, you were part of the task force."

"Yes. But it's not my case. My involvement with the task force was limited to providing operational support in Callipur. I tried, Shankar, but the commissioner refused. Let's wait till I hear back on the details that I have requested. They promised I will have everything by Friday, and we can read a copy of the interrogation report."

"Right, sir." Shankar was not happy, and Alok could sense that.

"Look, Shankar, let's see what the report says. If indeed it solves our case here or offers more clues, then we can follow up."

"Yes, sir. I do have some updates on our case. That can wait till tomorrow."

"Yes, let's do it tomorrow. Please don't forget, we still have to give Mishra-ji a report by Friday."

"Yes, sir."

By Friday, the alibis for all the workers had been checked. There was nothing much there to pursue. The Mathurs had given their statements. The interviews with Alok and Shankar were quick, and both were careful not to discuss Mrs. Rita Mathur's affair with rest of the family. The Mathur family had been home the entire night.

Harsh had come by and asked whether the Bhaskar brothers were still under suspicion. They were not. Mrs. Bhaskar, Pramod's wife, had given them a statement stating that she was in the club with friends the night of the incident, and that checked out. Alok had already told the rest of the officers in the station about the confession of the suspect in the robbery case regarding the Callipur murder. There was a general feeling that the gang of robbers was indeed responsible for Karan's death.

The only remaining item was for Shankar to visit the school to see if that offered any details. And then there was Shankar's private investigation into Manoj Yadav's whereabouts. He hadn't been able to get to either of these because he had been assigned to other duties at the port babysitting a state minister who was visiting for a week. He hated it, but security detail was something new police officers were tasked to do.

The only saving grace was that Nitya was on the minister's duty for the newspaper as well. That gave them an opportunity to talk. Alok had already told her about the link to the robbery case. She could sense from the conversation with Shankar that he wasn't convinced. Neither was she. But she liked the minster's visit, not because of the minister but because of Shankar. She enjoyed spending time with him and liked the fact that a young police officer was addressing her as *Nitya-ji*. She had repeatedly asked him to call her by her first name. Somehow, he didn't seem to get it. During many of these conversations, she got to know Shankar better and liked his company. She also unloaded her life on him, starting with her mother, Raj, her sisters, and her work. She found him to be attentive and curious. She decided to tell him about the letter in her desk.

"If I decide to take this job, then everything else falls apart."

"And if you don't?" Shankar asked.

"Then my life is mapped out for me by someone else, and they have guaranteed that that I will be happy."

"But you are not convinced."

"No," Nitya replied with a serious expression.

"Have you spoken to Raj about this?"

"No."

"Why not?"

"I don't know. Maybe because I just like to stall and don't make a decision unless I am forced to."

"Nitya-ji, the way I look at it, you have to make up your mind now."

"Yes. You are horrible at giving advice, and you are not helping. Did anyone tell you that?"

Shankar smiled back at Nitya.

"But you are right. Kavita said the same thing," Nitya said thoughtfully.

"I think you need to decide. It is important. You may regret your decision later, but you have to accept that."

"Is that your advice, Shankar? This mumbo jumbo doesn't mean anything. Just tell me what I should do. If I take your advice and it doesn't work out, then I will just blame you for the rest of your life, wherever you are. That's all. In any case, the new recruits leave after a year, and Alok told me you have requested a transfer. So, if you are not in Callipur, you don't have to deal with me for too long."

"Why did you ask Alok whether I had requested a transfer?"

"I don't know. You are changing the topic. We have to resolve my life first. What should I do? And don't tell me any more mumbo jumbo."

Shankar thought for a minute and smiled at her and said, "Make the more difficult choice."

"Why?"

"Because that's the one we don't usually make and regret later. That's what I would do. But it may not be the right one. We don't always know what the right choice is until much later. We know what's easy and what's difficult."

Nitya had become quiet after that. She liked these talks with Shankar.

"It's not the same for girls, you know."

"I know."

"Women have a much more complicated life. We have to deal with men and our mothers."

"Right. Not easy, I agree."

The other thing that had happened during the week was that Mrs. Chaturvedi had come to know Shankar really well from her window when he came to drop Nitya off. She had greeted him each time with a frown on her face and an expression of abject disapproval. She was happy when the state minister left.

Finally, Shankar found some time to go to the school in Callipur. He spoke to the principal and some of the teachers. He learned that Karan had graduated with modest grades. He had been good in sports and was involved in extracurricular activities.

"He was well liked by his teachers," the principal said.

"What about friends?"

"He had managed to make quite a few. You know, he came over from Sahibganj. It helped, of course, that there are some boys who came over from the same school. He managed to make new friends quite easily."

"No trouble or discipline-related issues?"

"None. In fact, he and his friends helped break up a couple of fights in school from escalating."

"What about Manoj Yadav? Was he friends with Karan?"

"Yes, they were. Manoj came over from Sahibganj as well."

The conversation with the other teachers painted the same picture of Karan.

The interrogation report from the robbery case that had been promised still hadn't arrived. The details were sketchy. Shankar had spoken over the phone with the officer in Ranipat who had questioned the suspect. But all he knew was that the suspect had been asked about several unsolved crimes in the area, including Karan's murder in Callipur. After being interrogated for hours and hours, he had confessed without providing any more details. Alok had sent the details of the confession to his superiors, and they considered the matter closed.

The following week, there was another labor strike, this time at the paper mill. Shankar, along with the other officers, had a hard time maintaining order in and around the mill. Thankfully, after two weeks, it ended.

There was some sad news as well. Professor Saumya Lal had passed away. They spoke to his doctor. Apparently, he had stopped taking his medication. Shankar and Alok went to the ceremony. It was a solemn affair. They had kept Mr. Lal informed of the investigation. He knew about the link to the robbery. There was no way of knowing whether he believed it or not.

With his death, the case seemed to be even more on the back burner. That was until Nitya's article in the paper and the summons from Judge Gita Shome for Alok and Shankar to appear in her chambers.

7

The Club

When Shankar arrived at work that day, there were not one but two notes in his office. Both were from Alok. He found that surprising. First, he could not recall the last time Alok had come to the station before he did in the morning. Second, both the notes said the same thing. *So, it must be serious*, Shankar thought.

He wasn't wrong. As soon as he entered Alok's office, the supervisor politely asked everyone else except Shankar to leave. He closed the door, asked Shankar to take a seat, and quickly settled in across from him.

"Judge Shome has asked us to appear in her chambers tomorrow," Alok finally said. Shankar knew he was worried.

"Why?"

"Have you read the papers this morning?"

"No, sir."

"Well, take a look, and tell me what you make of it." Alok handed the morning paper to Shankar and pointed to an article on the third page. It was written by Nitya about the robbery case. Most of it had to do with the facts surrounding that case. But there was a small paragraph questioning whether the police were right to link the robberies to Karan Lal's slaying. Shankar read the piece and for the most part agreed with it. It was well written, and he wondered why it created such a fuss. The papers were always questioning everything. That was their job, and this one didn't portray the police in a bad light, either. It merely raised the question whether the robberies had anything to do with Karan's murder. Shankar himself had his doubts.

When Alok spoke, Shankar realized what the summons was all about.

"Gita Shome is the judge in the robbery case. Do you know who she is?"

"Yes, sir."

Everyone in Callipur and especially at the club knew who she was. Gita was a trailblazer in her own right. She was one of the few women judges in India and only a handful in the state. She had a reputation of being no-nonsense, tough, but fair. She had been at the forefront of many landmark decisions in the state that had shaped the judicial system and its reach. She had resisted calls from the government during India's Emergency to pass laws curbing the freedom of press in the newspapers and radio. Hence, it was even more surprising that she would summon the police and the press to her chambers based on this article. Shankar had seen the judge quite a few times in the club. He had never spoken to her, but he knew that folks either liked or disliked her. No one who knew her seemed to have a neutral opinion about her.

"Let's get our stories straight on the case before we go to her chambers," Alok said.

"Yes, sir." Shankar could see that Alok was worried.

They spent the rest of the day reviewing both cases and rehearsing their responses to what the judge might ask. The next morning, before entering her chambers, Alok reminded Shankar of what he had said the previous day.

"Let me do most of the talking. If the judge asks you something, please respond clearly."

"Yes, sir."

When they entered the room, they could see the prosecution and defense lawyers from the robbery case. They also saw Nitya and the editor of *The Callipur Post* in the room as well. Alok and Shankar took a quick look around the room and seated themselves in the back. Shankar quickly glanced over to Nitya. She also had a worried look on her face.

When Gita Shome entered the room, everyone rose, and she quickly waved them to take their seats. It was a quick, short meeting where she did most of the talking. First, she turned her attention to Alok.

"What's this about the confession in the robbery case and the boy's death?"

"Your Honor, the police have reason to believe there could be a link between the two based on the suspect's confession."

"But it seems the confession was secured under duress. He was interrogated for hours, and now the defense is claiming that there is no firm link."

"Your Honor, that may well be the case. However, there is a possibility that the gang was operating in Callipur the same night, and they may have been involved with what happened to Karan Lal."

Broken Dreams: A Callipur Murder Mystery

The defense lawyers started to say something, but the judge immediately raised her hand to stop them. She looked at Alok and Shankar and said sternly, "I am the judge in the robbery case. From what I have heard so far, the police aren't sure themselves that there is a link. I am not concerned about the other case, but I hope that it is still open and you are continuing with the investigation. For now, I am ruling that this confession linking the two cases is inadmissible."

Then she turned her attention to Nitya and her editor.

"I am not in the habit of seeing my cases tried in the public domain in the print media."

"That was not our intent, Your Honor," Nitya said.

"God knows that we have just come out of a period where everyone was afraid to talk publicly, and I surely don't want to place any curbs on the Fourth Estate. But I also don't want readers getting the impression that the judiciary and police have already decided on who is guilty and how they should be judged."

"Understood, Your Honor."

"I expect the press to have some responsibility on how things are reported. I do want you to cover the case and offer your opinion freely in the editorials. But I don't want opinions to be reported as facts and news."

"Yes, Your Honor." Nitya nodded in agreement.

"Well, that's it, then. We will continue with the case in hand this afternoon. Thank you all for coming." They all got up and left her chambers.

In the parking lot, Alok went to have a word with the editor. That left Shankar and Nitya to talk about what had just happened.

"You got us into trouble, Nitya-ji."

"Did I? Maybe this means that Karan's case is still open, and you can still continue the investigation."

"I am not sure."

"Well, I am sure that I am going to get another dose of warnings from my editor."

"It was a good article," Shankar said.

"So, you didn't disapprove?" Nitya was surprised, and she looked at him.

"Not at all. You are right. Maybe I will be able to continue the investigation, even though the department may not put any more resources into it."

"Glad to see that I could be of some help."

"I do need your help with something," Shankar added, surprising her again. This was the first time Shankar had asked her for some assistance.

"With what? But before you answer, is it the police asking my paper for help with their investigation, or is it Shankar asking Nitya for help unofficially?" she asked with a sense of playfulness in her voice.

"It's Shankar asking Nitya unofficially," Shankar replied. "I need to know the whereabouts of one of Karan's friends during the night of his murder. It cannot be part of the police investigation since we don't have any witnesses, and the boy in question is not a suspect in any way. He is also well connected and is a friend from his previous school in Sahibganj."

"Is your investigation focusing on the schools now?" Nitya was curious.

"Not quite. I have already been to the school in Callipur. Maybe I will make a trip to Sahibganj, although at this point I am not sure if it will help in any way."

Nitya thought for a minute and replied, "I will help you under one condition. This stays between us, and we keep our bosses out of it for now. And if you do end up going to Sahibganj to visit his previous school, you will take me with you. All unofficial for now. I won't comment or write on any findings unless there is something concrete and we both agree."

Shankar agreed. They saw that Alok and her editor had finished their conversation. Shankar turned to Nitya. "When we can talk about this?"

"Come to the club in the evening. We can talk then."

"Sure," Shankar replied, then quickly headed off in the direction of Alok to find his car and get back to the station.

The Colonial Club in Callipur was more than one hundred years old. It was built by the British for the British. For the longest time before India's independence, Indians were not allowed inside the club—unless they worked there, of course. It was meant to be for British officers and their families stationed in Callipur and the adjoining towns. As time went by, the club started allowing members of the Indian Civil Service, and since India's independence, the membership was open to bureaucrats, officers, police, elected politicians, and their families. The membership of this group was automatic, but they had to pay for activities. The club was also open to members of the public, mostly businessmen, their families, and managers from the various industries in and around Callipur who could afford the hefty annual fees. All of Callipur's rich, famous, influential, and ambitious were club members. It was a place to conduct official business unofficially. It was also a place where people competed on how snobbish they could be. Everyone seemed to have an opinion on everything. Lack of knowledge was never an impediment to offer meaningless advice and lectures to whomever wanted to listen.

The club boasted of a decent library that had a good collection of books and even better subscriptions of magazines both Indian and foreign. It also had a swimming pool, badminton and tennis courts, three bars, two restaurants, multiple lounges, a big courtyard that doubled as a sitting area, and an open-air bar. The most popular parts of the club were the two bridge rooms, which had a constant stream of mostly gentlemen and some women playing cards, and the billiards room on the ground floor. It was difficult to find a free billiards table, although there were six in the club.

The club's grounds were massive. Huge gardens spread out in the front and the back, and the sprawling campus included two greenhouses with birds, including peacocks. The gardens and the pool were a hit among the children and young people. From the outside, the building looked like an old palace that hadn't changed much since it had been built. It was a white Colonial building, and the management made sure that it looked new with a fresh coat of paint each year.

On the inside, the decor was old and dark. The walls were filled with paintings of princes, rajas, maharajas, and their wives from another time. There were still a few paintings of British officers who were past presidents of the club. The rooms and the halls were decked with old wooden memorabilia of yesteryear, trophies, and photographs of past events. The club also organized social events and functions throughout the year and rented out its grounds for weddings and official ceremonies. The biggest annual event at the club was Diwali.

Being a police officer, Shankar had automatic membership. He went there mostly to play badminton, swim, and use the library. He had seen Gita Shome in the library. Sometimes he would hang out in the billiards room and at the open-air bar in the courtyard with his colleagues from work. He was there tonight looking for Nitya to engage her in finding out the whereabouts of the Yadavs. He looked around the room and saw Harsh coming towards him.

"I saw you, Alok, and Nitya at the courthouse today," Harsh said.

"Yes. Judge Shome had summoned us."

"How did it go?"

"Not too bad. We got scolded," Shankar said and smiled.

Harsh looked at him with a smile on his face. "Well, if you are here and in good spirits, then things went well. I am guessing it had to do with Nitya's article?"

"Yes."

"Good work on the robbery case, by the way," Harsh added.

"I wasn't involved in the case, but yes, it's a good thing we caught them," Shankar replied, and took another sip from his drink.

"I was sorry to hear about Professor Lal."

Shankar nodded. He saw Nitya walking towards them. Harsh waved at her to come over. They knew each other well. Nitya was close to Harsh's ex-wife, Rohini. That had helped in many ways. She could act as an intermediary when needed. The couple needed her during the divorce proceedings to ensure that the process was peaceful and amicable. Harsh was grateful for that. But that also meant that Mrs. Chaturvedi viewed Harsh with unrepentant suspicion. Now with Shankar in the picture, her focus and ire had shifted to him.

Shankar, Alok, and Nitya talked briefly about what happened in court that morning. Then Harsh and Nitya started talking about Akash, Harsh's son, who would be visiting during for a few days during the summer holidays and Diwali. Finally, some other lawyers whisked Harsh away for a game of snooker, and Nitya and Shankar were on their own.

"So, tell me, Shankar, what is it that you need help with?"

"The Yadavs and their whereabouts the evening of Karan's death," Shankar said.

Nitya blinked in surprise.

"Wow. I wasn't expecting that."

"It could be nothing, of course. It's probably nothing. But I could use your help."

"Well, I can understand why you don't want to do this officially. Hari Yadav is a big shot here. You are in luck. I know Mrs. Yadav, Hari's wife, really well. She is here in the club. I can ask her without raising any suspicions about where they were."

"Thank you, Nitya-ji. That will certainly help."

"But remember, if you go to Sahibganj, I am coming with you."

"Absolutely," Shankar replied.

As Nitya left to find out about the Yadavs, Shankar looked around and noticed the Bhaskars were in the club. They were engaged in conversation with another family. On the other side of the room, he could see Mishra-ji with Alok. He recognized a few more faces, though he didn't know them personally. Some mothers were scolding their children, and in the far corner, the Mathur family was starting to eat the food that they had ordered.

Harsh came back a few minutes later, and they started talking about music, movies, and cricket. The more Shankar spoke with him, the more he realized that Harsh was knowledgeable on many subjects and had an interest in collecting stamps and painting. Dr. Daphader soon joined them, lunging into a lecture on something called

DNA that confused Harsh and Shankar. But it seemed interesting, and the doctor gave them some insights on how he thought this could be used in the future by the police and the judiciary.

An hour went by, and Shankar finally saw Nitya emerge from the other side of the garden with a smile on her face. Shankar wanted to talk to her alone. He excused himself from the group and quickly walked up to Nitya. They walked over to the bar.

"Dead end, Shankar," Nitya said.

"What did you find?" Shankar asked.

"Hari Yadav was in the state capital on the night of the incident. He had left in the morning and hadn't returned until the next night. His wife had accompanied him."

"What about Manoj?"

"He was in Barrackpore that day. He and a friend, Ravi Pal, were attending a wedding that night. They had left the day before, attended the wedding, spent the night there, and came back the next morning. There's nothing there."

Shankar nodded his head in agreement.

Broken Dreams: A Callipur Murder Mystery

"The only other thing that might interest you is that both Manoj Yadav and Ravi Pal were Karan's friends from school in Sahibganj and in Callipur. I am not sure if that helps. In any case, they were both not in town that night and could not have been involved with all of this."

"Yes. I think you are right. Thank you so much." Shankar was impressed with how quickly Nitya had found all the answers from Mrs. Yadav.

"If you really want to know whether Manoj and Ravi were in Barrackpore that night, you can ask Harsh to help. He is from Barrackpore and could make some inquiries unofficially."

Shankar thought for a minute. The Bhaskars were no longer suspects in the investigation. He was the only one on the case, and the police department, for all intents and purposes, had concluded that the robbery gang was involved with Karan's death.

"Sure. Would you mind asking Harsh, Nitya-ji?"

"Another favor? Soon you will owe me big-time, and then you will be in real trouble. Of course, Shankar. I will ask him later tonight."

"Thank you."

"So, where does that leave you with the investigation? Only Sahibganj, if there's anything at all there that might help?"

"Yes," Shankar replied. Sahibganj was a long shot, but he decided that he would go anyway. Maybe being away from Callipur would help clear his thoughts.

They heard a crash, some raised voices and falling plates. It seemed that there was an argument between the Mathurs and the waiters. Something to do with the food. Before anything could happen, the manager had smoothed things over, and the Mathurs had been whisked away somewhere else.

"You know, people should know when to stop drinking," Nitya said, pointing to the commotion. Everyone was glad that it was over.

While he was lost in thought, Shankar could see Nitya waving at someone on the other side of the room. It was Mrs. Chaturvedi. *Oh God*. Shankar sighed She had seen them together again.

Nitya looked straight at him, smiled, and took a sip from her glass. "You know, my mother really, really doesn't like you. Like, at all. Just so you know."

"It must be my charming personality," Shankar replied.

Nitya couldn't help but laugh. Harsh, Dr. Daphader, and his wife soon joined them again. They spent the rest of the evening eating, drinking, and laughing.

Before leaving, Nitya took Harsh aside and told him about Shankar's request about Manoj and Ravi. Harsh agreed to look into it. He had enough contacts in Barrackpore to get their whereabouts, especially if they were attending a wedding. That could be done easily without raising any suspicion. Harsh was happy that his clients were no longer suspects.

The next time they met in the club was in a week's time for Alok Vij's farewell party. Alok's transfer to Delhi had finally come through. He and his wife were both very happy. It showed during their final visit to the club. Everyone was there. Mishra-ji raised a toast to Alok's contribution during his stint in Callipur. Shankar, for his part, thanked him for being a good boss. As he looked back at his time with Alok, he could never recall a moment where he had not been treated properly. Alok had given Shankar the latitude to investigate his cases. Whenever there was a situation that could get Shankar into trouble, Alok had warned him. He had also backed him up many times. He had given Shankar a great appraisal and spoke highly of him among his peers and his superiors. As Shankar looked at Alok, he wondered whether the general opinion about his now soon-to-be ex-boss was misplaced. Mishra-ji may have been a better officer and well liked among his peers. But he was also uncompromising and at times could come across as callous in dealing with the public. Alok, on the other hand, always strived to find a balance. He spoke nicely to and about everyone. He was ambitious, and in his playbook the way to go about doing that was to try to keep everyone happy. Shankar wondered which way his temperament would veer. Finding balance meant a constant struggle. Being self-righteous had its own set of issues.

Before leaving, Alok came by and wished Shankar well.

"I know you have put in a request for a transfer. Please feel free to get in touch with me if I can help in any way. Do look me up if you are in Delhi for anything. Bye, Shankar, and good luck."

Once the Vijs had left the club, Shankar decided to talk with Nitya and Harsh. Harsh found him first. Once they were all together, Harsh told them that he had checked up on the whereabouts of Manoj and Ravi. They were indeed at the wedding on the night of

Karan's death. Harsh also told them that he was going to Barrackpore to deal with some family matters and would reconfirm the same.

Shankar and Nitya then talked about when they could go to Sahibganj. It was not urgent, but he wanted to do it before the full force of the monsoon season set in. They quickly decided on a date and the arrangements. Until his new boss arrived, Shankar would be reporting to Mishra-ji, and getting his approval for a day trip to Sahibganj would not be a problem.

8

Monsoon

The rains came early that year. Indian monsoons are a wondrous event. Although Callipur was an industrial town, most of the surrounding areas were farmland. The city dwellers either loved the rain or hated it. The farmers prayed for it, and almost everyone needed it after the sweltering heat of the Indian summer. The forecasters were often wrong about the ferocity of the monsoon season, but they were usually right about how long it would last. The latest prediction was that it was going to be a long one with lots of rain. If there were no floods or waterlogging, most of the people went about their business. But everything seemed to take longer. Train journeys were no different. If the tracks were submerged, trains were delayed. But this was just the start of the season, and there had been no reports of heavy rains causing any major interruptions in the rail network.

Broken Dreams: A Callipur Murder Mystery

Shankar arrived early at the station. Malkhan had dropped him off at the station entrance, but he still had to navigate about a hundred meters before he could get to the covered part. A sea of black umbrellas in front of him tried to ward off the incessant rain that had started just as he was leaving the house. He often wondered why umbrellas were almost always black. For a country that was otherwise quite colorful, umbrellas always seemed to be black. In the Bollywood movies, everyone seemed to have a colored umbrella. But in real life, that was not the case. He preferred just his raincoat. It was much easier to navigate through a crowd, especially in the hustle and bustle of Callipur's morning rush.

He made his way to the platform, bought a ticket and a newspaper, and then headed straight to the tearoom to get a quick snack before the journey.

Luckily, he found a seat near the window, and as he sat down, he quickly gave his order to the waiter for tea and some biscuits. He had a small bag with a change of clothes, just in case he got drenched. He opened a copy of *The Callipur Post* and started reading. Most of the news was about the new cement plant that was to open in a few weeks. Preparations were under way to make it a grand event. There were articles about how many jobs the plant would bring. There was a full-page advertisement taken out by the local politicians on how Callipur was being heralded as a model town for a modern India. He quickly glanced at the weather forecast. No surprises there. It would be raining on and off with some sunny breaks. Then there was an article on rumors about an impending strike at the port. That certainly would not play well with the chief minster's visit and the cement plant's opening. Mishra-ji had already warned him that he, along with all his colleagues, would have to drop everything and make sure that law and order was maintained. All the more reason to get this trip to Sahibganj out of the way.

On the editorial page, there was an essay about how farmlands were being taken over to build houses, schools, and factories. It was a well-written piece. Although not directly, it seemed to insinuate a nexus between local politicians and businessmen to get land at cheap prices. He was convinced that this was a debate that would rage on not only in Callipur but also in other parts of India. He had read similar articles in the national newspapers about land being appropriated for development in the outskirts of big cities like Calcutta, Delhi, and Bangalore. In fact, one of his classmates was part of an investigation into one such incident in Bangalore. He wondered if Judge Shome was happy that she was retiring and not having to deal with such cases once more land was needed for the new plant to expand and house its workers. Development always seemed to be tied up with factories, housing colonies, and buildings. That wasn't going to change anytime soon.

One article caught his eye at the very bottom of the page. It was short and was written by his fellow traveler on this day. It was about the findings of a police commission that had been established to tackle corruption between forest officers and poachers in Sahibganj. The article questioned why it was taking so long for the government to implement the recommendations in the commission's report. It also questioned whether the various departments of the state government, including the police, were serious about tackling this crime, and whether instituting the commission itself was a ploy to delay enforcing any immediate actions. He reread the article, made some mental notes, and decided that he would ask Nitya about it during their journey.

He could hear that the rain had finally stopped. The drops no longer pattered against the tin roof of the tearoom. As he looked out of the window, he could see the sun trying to peek through the clouds. He could smell the rain, the water, and the soil, and it brought back memories from his childhood days when he would play with his friends and get drenched without a worry in the world.

Before putting down the newspaper, he quickly glanced at the last page, which was usually the sports section. There was an article about the Indian cricket team that would start a tour of England the following year. Some past Indian captain had done an analysis on how he thought the team might fare. Shankar was not an avid cricket fan, and in a country where cricket was a religion, that was a bit of an anomaly. Although he'd played the game occasionally during his school and college years, he never found the need to talk about it for hours on end with his colleagues or friends. He was interested, though, in following the performance of a short and talented batsman who had captured the imagination of the cricketing world with his ability to play fast bowling. He wondered how the player would fare under English conditions.

He checked the time and the handwritten timetable in the tearoom. There were only two trains departing that morning, and the Callipur-Calcutta Express was the first one leaving on another platform. Thankfully, it was on time. Once he had paid for his snack, he slowly started making his way to the train. He could see all the vendors trying sell all sorts of goodies to the travelers before they got on the train. He could also see the farmers bringing their produce in baskets getting on coaches specially reserved for them. He could smell all kinds of fruits, vegetables, spices, and tea.

He had taken off his raincoat and put it in his small bag. Being in uniform meant that very few people bothered him. As he made his way to his coach, he walked past the stationmaster, who gave him a quick nod. He checked his ticket and his watch. There was still about twenty minutes before departure, and he wondered where Nitya was. He was not worried about her not making the trip. She was very keen on going to Sahibganj. Without any delays, the journey should take a little less than three hours. It would be faster if the train ran on one of the new diesel engines that Indian Railways had introduced. But the Callipur-Calcutta Express was one of the remaining steam engines. Although they looked majestic, they were not as fast and efficient as the new diesel engines.

He was just starting to get a bit restless when he was relieved to see Nitya at the entrance of the platform a few hundred yards away. He waved at her, and she waved back. Someone had come to drop her off, and he immediately recognized the woman in a bright green sari with her. It was the loud and boisterous Mrs. Chaturvedi. He could tell that mother and daughter were exchanging words, and he quickly looked away towards the conductor, Mr. Dias, who had appeared at his side.

"Where to, Shankar sahib?"

"Sahibganj." He did not want to elaborate.

"Well, the rain has stopped, and the train is on time. We should get moving in no time."

Mr. Dias had seen the policeman wave at someone on the platform. He strained his neck to see who it was and noticed the young journalist.

"Not travelling alone, I see," Mr. Dias said, slightly amused.

"Not today, no. It is for work, and I will be back tonight." He really didn't want to continue this conversation and wondered what was taking so long for Nitya to make it to the coach.

Meanwhile, on the other end of the platform, Nitya was trying to end the discussion with her mother.

"I thought you were going alone. I didn't know you were going with another man."

"Mom, the other man happens to be a policeman. I would think that you would be happy that I will be safe with someone to watch over me."

"Yes, but he is not married. What will people think? What would Raj and his parents think if they knew this?"

"Why would they think anything at all? And I don't really care what they think. I really need to go. The train will be departing in a few minutes."

"When will this assignment come to an end? I thought this was all done!"

Nitya could sense the animosity in her mother's voice. She knew this would happen. That's why she wanted to come alone to the station. But her mom had insisted on dropping her off. Throughout the fifteen-minute ride, from her home to the station, Mrs. Chaturvedi had, once again, tried to impress upon her daughter the virtues of marrying early and pressed her about setting a date for the engagement and wedding with Raj.

"All that is very important and necessary to start the preparations," she had said. Nitya felt like her mother had started planning her wedding with Raj since she was a teenager.

She was not in a mood to argue any further. She quickly gave her mom a quick hug and told her that she would get dropped at home that night. There was no need to send the car. She gave her a smile to let her know that there was nothing she should be worried about. Mrs. Chaturvedi was not convinced but grudgingly made her way back to the car to go home.

Nitya was happy to see Shankar waiting at the platform.

"For a moment, I was worried that you would not be able to make it," Shankar said and quickly took her bag.

"Let's find our seats, and we will talk more."

Nitya's mother had given her a picnic basket with all sorts of sandwiches and snacks for the trip. She was constantly worried about her daughter getting sick from eating food from street vendors and railway canteens. She ended up with a bag and a basket and was only too happy that she could share some of that with her fellow traveler.

"It's a good thing the rain has stopped, and the train is on time."

"Yes," Shankar replied.

"When did you get here?"

"Awhile back. Force of habit. I was at the canteen getting a quick snack."

As they settled into their seats, the train started moving slowly, weaving its way out of the station. There weren't that many people on the train this morning. Most of the passengers were either going to Calcutta or were farmers taking their produce to Sahibganj. It was easy to find two window seats facing each other, and Nitya and Shankar settled in quite nicely without much ado. Travelling with a man in uniform, especially a policeman, had its rewards. No pesky vendors trying to sell their merchandise or passengers trying to strike up forced conversations. As the train reached the outskirts of the city, they could see the farmlands with the town receding in the background.

"So, Shankar, you got me into trouble again today with my mom."

"How so?"

"Well, she wasn't too happy that I am going to Sahibganj with a handsome-looking unmarried policeman."

That made Shankar blush slightly.

"I am sorry."

"Oh, don't worry about it at all. There's nothing anyone in the universe can do about making her happy. It's not your fault."

"I don't want in any way to be a reason for your familial disputes."

"Yeah, well, it's too late for that now, isn't it? The damage is done, and it's all your fault." She smiled and asked him about whether he had any news on who would be his new boss. They spoke about that and all the hoopla around the chief minister's visit. She told him that her boss had assigned her and two other colleagues to cover the visit and the plant's opening, and she wasn't too happy about that. Nitya looked outside. The skies were overcast, and it had started raining again. Shankar helped her in closing the shutters to prevent the rain from coming inside.

The train had picked up speed, and Callipur was no longer visible in the distant horizon. They started talking about the case.

"So, Shankar, the last time we spoke, you told me that you wanted to check out the school at Sahibganj. What exactly are you looking for? Don't worry; our conversation during the trip is entirely off the record. I won't report or publish anything unless it's something substantial. My readers have already lost interest in the case, and so has my boss. Most people believe that the gang of robbers killed Karan Lal. Karan's dad has also died. So, there's no one really following up on this with any sense of urgency."

Shankar thought for a bit before responding. She was right, for the most part. But not about the sense of urgency. It bothered him that she felt that way. He wanted to solve the crime whether it was on the public's mind or not.

"I am not quite sure. I guess I want to know if we have missed anything from his past that might throw some light into his death."

"You think the school has some answers."

"Maybe, maybe not. But I do want to find out if there's anything. It may not amount to much, but it is worth a shot. So, what is it exactly that you intend to find?" Shankar asked her.

"I want to find out whether there is any connection with the garage in Sahibganj that Pramod Bhaskar worked in."

Shankar had read about that in the file. But he didn't think much of it. It didn't even occur to him that there could be a connection. He was surprised that he had missed that. He was glad that Nitya was with him. She was sharp and intelligent. He liked that about her. She had also helped him with the case. So, it was good to have another pair of eyes looking at everything.

"Do you know where this garage is?"

"It's not far from the school." Nitya had been to Sahibganj before, and she had driven past it during her assignment there.

"We can go the school and then to the garage."

"Yes," Nitya responded. "The school is farther out. We can go there first and then to the garage on the way back to the station. Did you contact anyone at the school to let them know we were coming?"

"Yes, I spoke to the headmaster. I could sense that he wasn't too happy about it. But I told him it was about an ongoing investigation, and it wouldn't take very long," Shankar said.

He opened the window slightly to see if the rain had stopped. It was starting to get humid in the coach with all the windows shut.

"Let me ask you this. What is the one thing that has irked you about this case?"

"Everyone seems to have something to hide," Shankar responded right away.

"Yes."

"I guess small towns can be complicated."

"Tell me about it," Nitya said and sighed.

"You know, I was reading an article in the library in one of the foreign journals. It was written by a retired police officer in England. He wrote that if the solution to a crime or investigation is not obvious in the present, then it's probably because of something that has happened in the past," Shankar said thoughtfully.

"And that's why the visit to the school?"

"Doesn't hurt."

"No, it doesn't," Nitya agreed. "You really don't think that these gang of robbers had anything to with the boy's death? They had robbed the garage before."

"I looked at the crime scene on the very first night. It didn't look like a robbery. There was nothing that was taken. I read the files. Yes, the gang has been involved with other robberies in the area and with two assaults, one of which led to the death of a cycle shop owner in a neighboring village. But that seemed to have the hallmarks of a robbery gone badly. The victim had several defensive wounds, clearly indicating some sort of struggle. That's not the case here. The gang confessed to that killing but not this one. The confession that was obtained after the interrogation was sketchy at best. Yes, they had robbed the garage before. But why come back again? It doesn't make any sense."

"You know," Nitya said with smile, "I have been dealing with Callipur policemen for nearly five years now, and I must say that you are not like the others."

"Well, there are all kinds of people that end up joining the force from many different backgrounds. You shouldn't really put us all in the same bucket."

"I know, and now I won't after meeting you. You think about things, and you are thorough. I can't say the same for all your colleagues. How is your boss doing now?"

"Mishra-ji is biding his time and getting ready to retire. He is a good policeman but often misunderstood."

"Yes, I know."

She recalled how much Maheshwar Mishra had helped her in getting access to all the people and interviews for her article on the corruption in the forest department. She was convinced that he also wanted to get to the bottom of it and helped her uncover things that he couldn't pursue officially as part of the police force.

"Well, Nitya-ji, you have a bit of a reputation, too."

"Really, and what exactly is that?"

"That you are a hard-nosed, combative, and good reporter. You do want to find the truth, and you like to report both sides of the story."

"Wow, that's pretty direct. And what exactly do you think, Shankar? Am I all of that?" Nitya really wanted to know.

"I don't know. You are a good reporter and have helped me a lot. But I am not sure of the other stuff. I don't quite go with what other people have to say."

"And what is your opinion? Honestly?" Nitya asked.

"I think you are thorough. Your articles are well researched. I read the one on the nexus between the forest guards and poachers, and I thought it was great." Shankar remembered what he had read in the newspaper that morning. "I hope something good comes out of the commission report."

"What else?" Nitya asked now with a mischievous smile on her face. "I am sure you have come to some other conclusions about how I am."

"Only from what I have seen as part of the investigation and in the club."

"In the club?"

"Yes."

"What?" Nitya was now curious.

"You are opinionated and forceful while making your arguments. But when it comes to your relationship and upcoming marriage that everyone in the club seems to know about, you are coy and change the subject."

"Really? And you came up with all that while observing me at the club."

"I am a policeman. Force of habit. And you are doing it again."

"What?"

"Changing the subject," Shankar said and smiled.

"Well, there's one thing that irks me about you. It's that you call me *Nitya-ji*. I am not that much older than you. You have to drop the *ji* and just call me *Nitya*."

"All right, Nitya." Shankar smiled.

Nitya was amused and thoughtful at the same time. He was right. The whole marriage thing with Raj was the talk of the town, and she was fed up with it. Whenever it came up, she found a reason to find solace in her work or get away from home.

"Hungry?" she asked.

"Sure. Do you want me to order something?"

"No. First we have to finish the sandwiches that I got from home."

"Fine. I will get some tea," Shankar said as he got up and headed over to the pantry and placed his order.

While he was waiting, he looked out of the pantry window. The train was now chugging along quite nicely. He asked the pantry boy whether the train was on time, and he nodded. With two cups of tea and some biscuits, he headed back to his coach. He saw that Nitya had neatly placed some sandwiches on paper towels for them to eat. They were good. They talked a bit more about the case, rehashing what they had learned over the last few weeks. When they finished with the sandwiches and the tea, there was around half an hour left to get to Sahibganj.

Mr. Dias was doing his rounds, and when he came to their berth, they promptly handed in their tickets.

"Shankar sahib, the train stops in Sahibganj for only four minutes. Please be ready, and don't forget to take all your belongings. Who is this lovely lady traveling with you?" He looked at Nitya, awaiting some sort of introduction.

"This is Nitya Chaturvedi. She is a reporter with *The Callipur Post*, and we are going to Sahibganj as part of a story and investigation."

"Nice to meet you. Are you Akhilesh Chaturvedi's daughter? I am acquainted with your father. We play cards sometimes at the club. He is quite a good bridge player. I thought I saw Mrs. Chaturvedi at the platform."

"Yes, she was dropping me off." Nitya sighed.

"Well, have a nice day, then. I hope you stay out of the rain. I hate the monsoons. The water gets into my bones."

Not as much as people like you, thought Nitya. She looked up at Shankar in exasperation and just resigned herself to how this encounter would be recounted among her father's friends. It would set off all sorts rumors about her and Shankar.

As they looked outside, they could see that the paddy fields had changed into wooded forests with houses scattered in the distance. As they approached the station at Sahibganj, Shankar and Nitya both took hold of their belongings. The picnic basket was already on its last leg. She left it with the pantry boy. As they alighted from the train into the platform, they were glad that the rain had stopped, and it was sunny.

Shankar had made arrangements with one of his classmates to get him a vehicle. There was a young driver at the station with a placard. As soon as he saw Shankar in uniform, he made his way through the crowd and immediately took hold of their bags and belongings.

"Raman Singh, sir! Vinay-sir has sent me to be with you, and I am at your service all day."

"Nice to meet you, Raman. This is Nitya, and she will be with us as well."

"Good morning, madam."

"Good morning, Raman."

"Where to, sir?"

"First stop is Sahibganj Memorial School."

9

Sahibganj

Sahibganj was a small town. It used to be an old British outpost before India's independence. There was an old army hospital that had since been converted into a vocational college and training institution for all kinds of workers. The government had set up the institute to train factory workers, mill workers, miners, and mechanics, hoping that one day it would grow into a technical college or institute of some repute. It had failed spectacularly.

Like many ill-conceived government projects, this one had started with a lot of pomp and show, but then people quickly realized that unless there were industries in the vicinity where people could find jobs, no one would come. Callipur was the nearest industrial town, and it had its own training facilities, plus the industries made sure that their workers were trained on the job.

Over time what remained of the institute was an abandoned shell of a building. There were some talks of selling the land and the building to create a hotel or a resort. After all, Sahibganj was in the middle of a forest with lots of exotic plants and animals and, if developed properly, could attract a lot of tourists.

Nitya recalled her last visit to Sahibganj. On the way to the school, she told Shankar how she had investigated the forest officers and politicians. She also mentioned how Maheshwar Mishra had helped her with the investigation, made sure that she had adequate protection during her visits to Sahibganj, and had complimented her profusely when the article was published. Shankar listened to all of this with great interest and was happy to hear that about his boss. He often felt that Maheshwar was viewed in a bad light through no fault of his own.

As the rickety Jeep made its way through the village roads, they got a clear look at Sahibganj. Surrounded by forests on all sides, it is was a pretty town. Apart from the abandoned institute, there were some bungalows for the people who worked in the forest service. There were two small hotels catering to tourists, who mostly came from either Calcutta or Callipur. There was a small police outpost, a health clinic that catered to the local population, a small bazaar selling food and local crafts, and then the school.

The Sahibganj Memorial School was well known throughout India. It used to be the residence of the maharaja of Callipur, who was rumored to have many mistresses. The secluded palace in the midst of a forest town had been the perfect getaway for a luxurious, wasteful life. The maharaja had been educated in England, and when he came back to India after a decade, it was a completely different country than the one he had left. The princely estates had a tough time keeping their past glory, and most of the land now belonged to the government. The maharaja had decided to convert this palace into a school and had created a trust to save it from being usurped by the local government.

Making it an educational institution made it difficult for anyone to take the land. But what really saved the school were the families of the students who went there. It was a private all-boys residential school. The fees were steep. The tuition and lodging for a year at the school was more than what most Indians earned during the year. While the maharaja was alive, he made sure that other royal families would send their boys to be educated there. After his death, the ownership was transferred to the trust that was owned and managed by parents of the enrolled students.

The school's clientele had changed dramatically over the years. Now most of the students were the sons of the builders of modern India: the industrialists, businessmen, and politicians. There were still some royal families who had managed to invest wisely and were able to hold on to their wealth but not their past glory. The parents made sure that the reputation of the school was always good and intact. Any sort of malicious article or incident was quickly hushed up. The owners of most of the newspapers sent their boys to the same school. They had no intention of slinging any mud on its activities. That said, the school was run well. Except for a few incidents where the offending boys were promptly expelled and the situation "managed" with their parents, the students seemed to enjoy their time there. Over the years, many of the graduates had decided to send their boys there. A well-rounded education seemed to be the school's de facto motto.

There was another very small group of students who could get admission to the school. They were the sons of teachers and staff. The trust managing the school had decided that this was the only way they could attract good teachers and staff. This is how Karan Lal gained admission to the school. His father, Professor Saumya Lal had been a respected teacher in the school. He had taught there for almost twenty years. By the time he retired, he was head of the science department and was regarded highly by the members of the trust and his students. Karan had spent most of his school years there before moving with his father to Callipur. The trust had made an exception to allow Karan to complete his studies in the school, but he had declined because he wanted to move with his father.

As the Jeep slowly turned onto the road leading up to the school, Shankar and Nitya were impressed by the sprawling campus. The gates were majestic, and once the Jeep entered the school grounds, they were in a different world. The beautiful gardens that led up to the main building seemed like something out of a photograph. The lawns on either side were full of students eating and chatting. The main building had been renovated many times, and it resembled a beautiful, well-maintained palace. Farther afield, they could see the sports grounds filled with students playing cricket and soccer. Beyond the sports grounds was the boarding house for the students, the teachers' mess, and the staff quarters.

"The grandeur of this place is better than even the Indian Police Academy," Shankar said.

"Yes. It is impressive," agreed Nitya.

The Jeep came to a halt in one of the parking spots reserved for guests. Before heading to the main building, Shankar turned to Raman Singh. "Raman, we are leaving our bags and belongings here. We will be here for a couple of hours. I hope that's fine."

"Yes, sir. Don't worry. I will be waiting here for you and madam."

As they walked up to the main building, someone who looked like an office clerk met them.

"Hello, sir, madam. My name is Prakash Rao. I am the headmaster's secretary. I will be escorting you during your visit to our campus."

"Thank you, Mr. Rao. I am Shankar Sen, who spoke to you on the phone to arrange the visit, and this is Nitya Chaturvedi, a reporter with *The Callipur Post*. We are on a tight schedule and will be catching the train back in the evening. Please lead the way. We want to first meet the headmaster, if you don't mind."

"Sure," Rao responded eagerly and led them through a long corridor towards another building connected through a courtyard.

"Why are all the students outside?" asked Shankar.

"You arrived during recess. You will be hearing the bell in a few minutes, and then they will all be heading back to their classrooms."

They walked past the courtyard and arrived at the headmaster's office.

"Sir, madam, please wait here. I will let Mr. Tripathi know that you are here. It may take a few minutes until recess is over."

"That's fine," Shankar responded. "Can you show me to the men's room, please?"

"Sure. There's one down the hallway just past the water fountain. You won't miss it."

"Thank you."

As Shankar made his way down the hallway, Nitya sat down on the comfortable sofa in the waiting area and started leafing through the school brochures and magazines. They were full of articles of the school's glorious past and its reputation. As she looked beyond the waiting room, she noticed many boys lined up in a small corridor leading up to the headmaster's office. They were all eagerly looking at her, smiling and passing comments between themselves. Teenage boys in a boys' school— she could only imagine what they could be talking about. She got up and headed to the wall across the waiting area. There was a glass enclosure full of awards and trophies that the school had won in various sporting events. As she was reading some of the inscriptions, Shankar returned and was standing beside her.

"What do you think?" he asked.

"Impressive school. Great campus. I can't say how it does academically. Most of the awards here are for sports. What about your first impressions?"

"Same as yours, plus a few more things," Shankar replied.

"Such as?"

"A place that will guard its reputation at all costs. Full of secrets. Things to hide."

"Are you always this suspicious of everything?"

"I am a policeman. Force of habit. Part of the job."

"Ah yes. I had forgotten about that." Nitya smiled, and they both turned to see that the secretary had now returned. They heard the recess bell, and they could hear the kids in the corridor heading back to their classes.

"The headmaster will see you now."

"Thank you, Mr. Rao."

They entered the office through the large heavy doors. It was a huge room with a large desk all the way at the end near a majestic window. Near the door was a sitting area, and between that and the desk, were some bookshelves filled with more school trophies and awards. On the opposite end was a small coffee table with some chairs. Everything about the room was old, dark, and intimidating. And so was the headmaster.

"My name is Suman Tripathi. I am the headmaster of this school." He turned to face Shankar and continued. "The commissioner told me that you were coming. But he didn't tell me that you were bringing a reporter with you."

They could sense the animosity in his stern voice. Nitya tried to put his fears to rest as much as she could.

"Sir, my name is Nitya Chaturvedi, and I am here because of a general interest in the case. I have no desire to write about the school or anything that may show the school in a bad light."

The headmaster seemed somewhat assured. Although he did not smile, his voice became calm.

"The school's reputation will remain intact no matter what you may or may not write, Ms. Chaturvedi. We value the privacy of our students and staff and will go to great lengths to keep it that way. We do not allow outsiders to visit the school without a specific reason or recommendation. I agreed to this visit because the commissioner assured me your investigation had nothing to do with the school itself, and you were interested in getting more information on one of our former students and a staff member."

"Please, sir, I understand. That's exactly why we are here. Please don't worry on my account."

"What is it that you want to talk about?" He turned to Shankar.

"We are here to inquire about one of your students. He was the son of one of your professors, the late Mr. Saumya Lal. As you may know, he also died a few weeks ago."

"Yes. I knew Mr. Lal quite well. He was a very good professor. The students loved him, and we missed him dearly once he moved to Callipur after retirement. It was very sad indeed to hear about Karan's untimely death. I am sure it wasn't easy on the professor, and I suspect that may have hastened the inevitable. He wasn't keeping well, you know. He had a heart condition and had a few stints at the hospital."

"Yes, sir. We wanted to know if you could tell us a bit more about Karan," Shankar continued.

"Karan?" The headmaster was surprised. "He was a good boy. Not strong academically but very nice. He really took very good care of his father and his condition. You know, we offered that he could stay on to finish his studies after his father's retirement, but he refused. They decided to move to Callipur to be near the hospital for his treatment. Karan was a good, responsible kid. I did not interact with him much, but from what I heard from my staff, he seemed like the kind of boy who put duty above all else. I can't say that about all the boys in his generation."

"What about his friends and interests outside of school?" Shankar asked.

"I can't say really. Well, his class has already graduated. Most of his friends are no longer in the school. But there are a couple of teachers who knew him well, and he was into sports. You can ask Mr. Vinod Kumar. He is our physical education teacher, and he probably knew him better than anyone else since Karan was part of the soccer team."

"That would be great." Shankar looked at Nitya to see if she wanted to ask any questions. She didn't. "If we think of anything further, we will ask you on the way out. Thank you."

Mr. Tripathi got up and said, "I am sure you and Ms. Chaturvedi haven't had lunch. Mr. Rao will take you to the teacher's mess. You can eat something there, and I will make arrangements for Mr. Kumar and a couple of other teachers to meet you there."

Before Nitya could object, Shankar turned to the principal and nodded. *How much can this guy eat?* Nitya wondered. *He just finished off a slew of sandwiches less than than an hour ago, and he is hungry again?*

But as she approached the teacher's canteen, she realized why Shankar wanted to go there. He had seen the school layout and map. The canteen was at the very end of the school, past the courtyard, the main building, and grounds area. It would give them a good idea of how the school looked from the inside. As they walked through the corridors, they could see inside the classrooms, the library, the science lab, and the gym. The canteen was right next to the gym. As they descended to the common area reserved for teachers, they could see the pictures of students from various teams and classes from earlier years hanging on the walls.

They already saw two teachers in the room and easily recognized one of them as the gym teacher. Vinod Kumar was a retired cricketer. He'd never made it to the national team but was good enough to represent his home state in domestic matches for a few years. Following his retirement, he had taken up a job at the school. He had come highly recommended by one of the members on the board, and that pretty much clinched the job for him over everyone else. He knew Karan quite well.

"He was a good boy and was good enough to be part of the soccer team. In fact, he was a reserve player. But he got his chance to play after a couple of players got injured after a brawl. You know how team sports are and how teenage boys can be competitive. Anyhow, once he got his chance, he excelled and was a regular part of the starting lineup."

"Was he friends with Manoj Yadav and Ravi Pal?" Shankar asked. Mr. Rao's ears perked up, and he strained his neck from the far side of the room to hear the conversation. He knew who Manoj Yadav and Ravi Pal were. Their names hadn't come up during the conversation with the headmaster.

"Not particularly. His circle was different. He mostly hung out with the children of the other members of staff at the school."

Not surprising, Shankar thought. That would make sense. He probably did not have much in common with all the other rich kids. Sons of the staff members were probably more down to earth like him. They spoke a bit more about Karan and his father. They learned that the boy was good in extracurricular activities. What struck Shankar as odd was a comment that Vinod made about Karan intervening to stop some fights and brawls at school. He had heard the same comment about Karan from the principal of the school in Callipur.

The other two teachers also painted a similar picture. An overall nice boy, not strong academically, good soccer player, loved cars, doted on his father, took care of him, and loved listening to music. As they finished with all the interviews, Shankar asked Vinod Kumar if he could go to the gym and look at some of the pictures from Karan's class.

"I don't see any issues with that. Mr. Rao?"

Before Mr. Rao could offer any sort of objection, Shankar had already entered the gym and started looking at the pictures hanging on the walls. Nitya had joined him. The photos were all arranged by year, so it was easy to find the class pictures from 1975. That was when Karan had finished the tenth grade and had moved to Callipur. There was a picture of the soccer team. In another one from his grade, although it was hazy, they could recognize Karan and Ravi. Manoj was probably there, too, but they couldn't make out the faces of all the boys in the back row.

It was the next picture that completely shook them up. It was a photograph of all the staff and their children. Shankar spotted him first, the boy standing next to Karan. Nitya almost gasped when she saw him in the picture. They looked at each other and for almost a minute were absolutely speechless.

The silence was broken by a pleading voice from Mr. Rao.

"Are there any more pictures you would like to see?" There was something in his voice that was almost urging them to leave the room.

Shankar ignored Mr. Rao completely and looked at Vinod Kumar and the other teachers.

"What about this boy standing to next to Karan?"

"Oh, yes, he was a good friend. But he got into trouble. Something wrong with the kid, I think. Lots of temper tantrums and physical altercations with students. He ended up in the clinic a couple of times to get stitches. There was another incident with a boy where they both ended up in the hospital with head injuries. Finally, during one of the other incidents, he lashed out at a teacher. That was the last straw for Mr. Tripathi."

Shankar looked at Vinod and chose his words carefully. "The fights that Karan tried to break up. Did they involve this boy?"

"Yes. They were good friends."

Shankar turned to the other teachers and pointed to the boy standing next to Karan in the photograph.

"Oh yes. Bad news, that boy," said one of the other teachers.

"He beat up a kid from sixth grade once just because he wouldn't share his lunch with him." The other teachers looked at Vinod and nodded in agreement.

"What happened after that?" Shankar asked.

"His father was a member of the staff," Vinod responded.

"Yes. We see him in the picture, too." Shankar had recognized him instantly.

"The boy had to be expelled. His father was asked to leave as well, and I think they ended up moving to Callipur. I don't know anything after that."

"Thank you. You have been most helpful."

The teachers had all the left the room, and Shankar and Nitya were staring at the photograph again with Mr. Rao trying to gauge what on earth could be so intriguing about a picture from 1975 with the staff and their children.

"Mr. Rao, we would like to take this picture with us as part of our investigation. We will return it to you after making a copy for our records," Shankar said with a polite, firm voice.

"I am not sure. I would have to check with the headmaster."

"Certainly. Perhaps you can also mention that if we do leave without the photograph, we would have to let the commissioner know that we will be seeking a warrant to search the school premises not only for this photograph but also for other things that we may find. I am sure that it won't do much for the well-guarded reputation of this school if it were to come out that police have been looking for clues inside the campus related to the murder of an ex-student. All we are asking is that we take this picture, make a copy, and return it as is."

"I will just check," Mr. Rao said and hurried to find a phone.

Broken Dreams: A Callipur Murder Mystery

"Understood," Shankar said, politely holding on to the photograph firmly.

As Mr. Rao left the room to check with the headmaster, Nitya stood very close to Shankar.

"Well played. Do you think it will work?"

"We will see." If it didn't, Shankar was out of ideas. It was a complete bluff. He couldn't go the commissioner, asking him to apply for a warrant. There were absolutely no grounds to ask for one. In fact, he was more likely to get scolded for even bringing it up.

Mr. Rao made a quick phone call to the principal's office from the adjoining room and returned to let Shankar and Nitya know that the school had no objection whatsoever. The headmaster had just requested that the photograph be returned as quickly as possible.

"Certainly." Shankar was relieved. Nitya wanted to burst out laughing.

"Would you like to get some lunch at the canteen?" Mr. Rao asked very softly, hoping that they would refuse.

"Not really. I think we will probably head back to our car. We still have two more stops to make in Sahibganj before leaving for Callipur. Please do thank Mr. Tripathi on our behalf for letting us visit the campus and helping us with our inquiries."

"I certainly will." Mr. Rao was relieved to see them get in the Jeep and drive towards the campus gates. He hurried back to the headmaster's office to give him a detailed account of what had transpired. But once Mr. Tripathi heard everything, he couldn't make any sense of it at all.

They made two more stops. One at the clinic to check the records to see if indeed the boys had been treated there following their altercations and to get the nature of their injuries. The clinic confirmed all the visits, and although they could not provide any details, they gave enough to indicate the seriousness. Shankar and Nitya also learned that the school had actively intervened with the parents and medical staff at the clinic to not report the incidents to the police. *All to protect the school's reputation*, Shankar thought.

The next stop was the garage where Pramod Bhaskar had worked before moving to Callipur. There was no big revelation there. Pramod was a good worker but never saw the job as a long-term career. They did confirm that he had a hand injury that prevented him from doing many things. He always wanted to move to be closer to his brother and eventually wanted to his son to take over the family business in Callipur.

Once they were all done, both Shankar and Nitya were famished. It had been quite an eventful day, and they had finally figured out what likely happened that night. They decided to head to the station. Once they arrived, they let go of Raman Singh.

"You have been very helpful, Raman. I will let Vinay know for sure." He gave him a hefty tip that Raman grudgingly accepted.

There was a small tea stall at the Sahibganj train station with a covered waiting area. They figured they would eat something there and discuss what had happened during their visit. By the time they arrived at the station, there was about an hour left for the train back to Callipur. They quickly checked with the stationmaster. The train was on time. Shankar asked whether there was a public phone booth. Thankfully, the phone lines had not been affected by the rains. They decided to call Harsh and have him meet them at the King's restaurant that night once they returned. He was driving back from Barrackpore and would be in Callipur by now.

"We have some news that we want to share with you right away," said Shankar over the phone.

"Same here," said Harsh. "Both Manoj Yadav and Ravi Pal were in Barrackpore the night of the murder. They were identified by lots of folks at a wedding. Some of them are my relatives. They are not involved with what happened that night."

"We know," Shankar replied.

Harsh could make out from his voice that Shankar had solved the case, or at the very least had a good idea of what happened that night. He also didn't want to press him for answers over the phone.

"I will meet you at the King's restaurant at nine p.m. Do you want me to pick you and Nitya up at the station? It's only a few minutes away."

"No. I have already arranged for Malkhan to pick us up."

Shankar then placed another call, this time to the telephone exchange. He requested some phone records and asked them to be delivered to the police station next morning.

After a quick meal, Shankar and Nitya boarded the train and during the journey tried to get their head around why they had missed something so obvious.

"I think it comes back to what you said before, Shankar."

"What's that?"

"If you can't solve a crime with what you see in the scene or what's happening in the present, you have to start taking a look at what has happened in the past."

"Right."

10

Callipur

The rest of the journey back to Callipur was uneventful. It had started to rain again, but they were too excited to notice. They talked a great deal about the school, the types of students who went there, and whether indeed it offered a well-rounded education as the school motto seemed to suggest. They also talked about their own schools and their teachers. Although they came from totally different parts of India, they had quite a lot in common.

As the steam locomotive hissed and heaved into Callipur station, Shankar could see his trusted aide and driver, Malkhan Dogra, waiting for him on the platform. He quickly gave him his and Nitya's bags and asked him to take them to the King's restaurant.

Harsh was already waiting at the restaurant when they arrived. He had made sure that he had a found a booth in the corner that was secluded and somewhat isolated from the noise of all the other patrons. It wasn't that crowded, anyway. The incessant rains had a put a damper on what would otherwise have been a busy night.

"Hi, Nitya. Hi, Shankar. It seems you may have solved the puzzle," Harsh said as they sat down.

Nitya nodded and turned to Shankar.

"Just show him the photograph."

"What photograph?"

Shankar took out the picture and gently placed it on the table.

"This is a photograph of all the staff and their children who were enrolled in the school in 1975."

Harsh started focusing on the picture with great intensity. He immediately recognized Karan and Saumya Lal. Then his face changed. Nitya looked at Shankar, and they both knew that he was starting to make the connection. They told him about the temper tantrums, the fights, the head injuries and stitches, the visits to the clinic and hospital.

"I guess you might have just solved this mystery." Harsh was impressed.

"I think we are programmed to look at the sons of politicians and industrialists. Well, now we know that in this particular case, they are not involved." Nitya was right, and they both nodded in agreement.

"The only problem I see is that we have no evidence, circumstantial or otherwise, related to this crime. There are no witnesses either." Shankar was right.

He turned to Harsh and asked, "In the absence of any witnesses or evidence, what can we possibly do?"

Harsh took some time before replying thoughtfully. "The only way is to make him confess. If he doesn't or asks for a lawyer, you can't really do much. You cannot interrogate him. There isn't much to go on. If the lawyer tells him to keep quiet, as he is legally entitled to do, you can't charge him with anything. His alibis were his family members. They won't change their testimony, and you can't charge them with falsifying their statements without any witnesses. You have nothing to challenge them on. The only way forward, from what I can see, is if he confesses."

"So, what do we do then?" Nitya asked.

"I think Shankar needs to go talk to the family and make it sound like it's part of the regular investigation. Then lead into what may have happened that night. If they decide not to cooperate, there's not much else that can be done from a legal standpoint."

They all realized that would indeed be quite challenging.

"I need to talk to my boss tomorrow morning to let him know what we uncovered. I can then go and meet the family," Shankar said.

"I can come with you," Nitya added quickly.

"I am not sure that's a good idea. I think they might tighten up even more knowing there's a reporter present. On the other hand, if you were to come, we could make it sound like we had some questions following our visit to the school. I don't know. Let me think about it and talk to my boss. I will let you know by ten tomorrow morning."

Harsh agreed with Shankar's plan. "Now let's enjoy some good food. I have ordered already. I got tired of waiting. I am not sure what you like. So, I ordered everything I like, and I am hoping that you will like it, too." They all smiled.

They spent the rest of the evening eating, drinking, and discussing their trip. They recounted in detail what had happened at the school. Harsh listened to every word religiously. Nitya called her mom from the restaurant to let her know that she was back in Callipur. Both Harsh and Shankar graciously offered to drop her home. But she recalled what had happened that morning when her mom had realized that she was going to Sahibganj with an unmarried policeman. She asked her mom to send the car to come pick her up at the restaurant. This gave her some more time to talk about the eventful day with Harsh and Shankar. Once the car arrived, they came outside to see her off and went back inside to finish their meal.

"Both of you did well today, Shankar. Something tells me that you enjoyed the trip as well. That's good," Harsh said.

Shankar arrived at work early the next morning to talk to Maheshwar Mishra. On his desk were the phone records he had requested from the telephone exchange the day before. He knew his boss was always busy. It was easiest to catch him during the first hour in the office. He was excited to let him know what had happened during the eventful trip to Sahibganj.

As Shankar recounted what had happened the previous day, Maheshwar listened to him without interruption.

He looked at Shankar with a pensive expression on his face. Shankar could only guess what his boss was thinking.

"The main problem will be proving any of this. You do realize that, don't you?"

"Yes, sir."

"The only way is to bring the boy and his family in for questioning and see if he confesses."

"I was going to go there today. I was thinking of taking Ms. Nitya with me."

"Hm," Mishra-ji said, lost in thought. He then nodded his head. "Yes, Shankar. That may be a good idea. You could go there and see if they are receptive to coming in for a police interview. Taking Nitya might put them at ease. But if they decide to come in, then we will have to do it by the book. The boy needs to have legal representation and no reporters."

"I agree, sir."

"Well, good luck, then. You did well, Shankar. Remember, not a word of this to the commissioner unless you manage to get a confession. This is all speculation at this point. The official line still is that the gang of robbers most likely did this. There is nothing to suggest anything else."

"Understood."

As he left the office, Maheshwar realized that Shankar was turning out to be a good investigator. He started sifting through all the papers and files at his desk, looking for all the forms he needed to fill out before his upcoming retirement in a few months.

Shankar made his way back to his office and called Nitya. He was dreading whether Mrs. Chaturvedi would pick up the phone. Luckily, she didn't, and it was Nitya's voice on the other end of the line.

"Hello! Good morning, Shankar. I have been waiting for your call. So, what's Mishra-ji's take on all of this?"

"We have to tread carefully and not make it sound like a police questioning. We have to try to convince them to come in for an interview and see if they want to revise any part of their statements."

"That will be difficult."

"Yes," Shankar replied.

Nitya knew he was worried.

"When were you thinking of heading over there?"

"In an hour or so. Do you want me to pick you up on the way?"

"No. I will ask the driver to drop me off at the station," she said.

"I will be in my room looking through the case files one more time."

"OK. I will see you soon."

Shankar spent the rest of the hour going through all the interviews and statements from the family. He called the principal at the school in Callipur to ask him some questions on some incidents in the past where Karan had stepped in to stop fights. He had sent and received some telegrams in the morning to other police stations to ascertain the family's background. The picture was becoming clearer with each new detail. A family with a troubled boy with mental issues. Violent fits of rage. Fights and brawls in school with some children ending up in the hospital with serious injuries. A cover-up by the family and the school at Sahibganj. Moving from place to place with a hope that a new environment would make things better. As he was going through the call logs and phone records from the exchange, his telephone rang. It was his classmate Vinay from Sahibganj.

"Hi, Shankar. It's a pity that you only came for a day. We couldn't spend any time together."

"Yes. We were in a hurry. You know how it goes. Your man Raman did a grand job taking us around."

"Well, next time, you have to stay over, and we will go hiking in the woods."

"Sure."

"I have the medical files that you have requested. All unofficially, of course."

"Understood."

"I will send them over to you. I looked at them, and honestly, they are quite technical with all sorts of medical terms. You will need a doctor to go over them and explain these in plain English."

"Thanks, Vinay. That's a great help. I will send Malkhan over tomorrow to Sahibganj to get the files from you. Tell me something. When you went over the files, what is your first impression? Anything that stood out?"

"A troubled boy with mental issues. It seems the family did try to get him treated. It seemed to have worked for a while and then made matters worse."

"Thanks again for your help, Vinay. I owe you one. When you come over next time, we will go to the club. Everything's on me."

"Deal."

"Bye."

As he hung up, Shankar recalled his time with Vinay at the police academy. Vinay came from a business family. They did not want him to pursue a career in the police service. He resisted. He was a good student, did well at school, and excelled at the academy in almost everything. As he was arranging the rest of the papers at his desk, Malkhan barged in. He had repeatedly told him, at times quite sternly, to knock but to no avail.

"Nitya madam is here, sir."

"Please send her in. We will be leaving soon."

"Yes, sir."

Shankar cleared off his desk and told Nitya what he had heard from Vinay regarding the troubled boy.

"I guess it all fits," Nitya said.

"Yes."

"But still no evidence, no witnesses."

"Right. Shall we?"

"Sure." They walked through the long corridor of the Callipur police station, then across the courtyard to the parking lot. Most of the people in the station knew Nitya. She had been there to follow up on various news stories. They tried to avoid her as much as possible. It was all the more reason for them to wonder what she was doing with Shankar Sen. Once they got to their car, Malkhan opened the door for them and got into the driver's seat.

"Where to, sir?"

Shankar handed him the address.

"I have a job for you, Malkhan. You have to go to Sahibganj tomorrow to get some files for me. I will give you the details when we are back at the station."

"Sure, sir."

"You can take the train. I will get the station to approve the expenses."

Malkhan was happy. He liked train journeys. He liked Shankar, too. He always treated him with respect and wasn't like the other officers. He wondered, though, why he was going to the Mathur residence and why was Nitya with him this morning.

During the short drive, Nitya and Shankar decided how they would play it. As both Maheshwar and Harsh had suggested, they would try to make it seem like it was a follow-up visit to get more details after learning a few things during their trip to Sahibganj the day before. The idea was to somehow convince the family to come to the station for an interview with Rajesh.

As they arrived at the Mathur residence, they could see that the family had just finished breakfast and were lazing around in the courtyard. A servant met them at the door.

"We have to come to see Mr. Swaroop Mathur."

"He is not in," replied the servant, "but he should be back soon. He has gone out for a short walk."

"Is Mrs. Rita Mathur or Rajesh in?"

Rita Mathur had seen them approach and walked over with her sister in-law. She remembered Shankar from his previous visit. She also recognized Nitya from the club and had spoken to her a few times.

"How can we help you?" Rita asked with a worried look on her face.

"We were wondering if we could speak to Rajesh."

"Why?"

"We just came back from Sahibganj and were wondering if he could help us in giving us a few more details about the school there," Shankar said, choosing his words carefully.

Their expressions turned sullen at the mention of Sahibganj. The two Mathur women looked at each other. There was moment of complete silence.

"Talking to Rajesh will not be possible. He has left for England. We sent him to London for higher studies. But our husbands will be back soon, and you can speak to them."

"Sure," Shankar replied.

"Please take a seat. Would you like to have some water or tea?"

"Water would be fine, thank you," Nitya said.

As they waited, both Shankar and Nitya realized that if indeed the boy had been sent to England, there was not much they could do. After a few minutes, two gentlemen entered the room.

"I am Swaroop Mathur. I am Rajesh's father. This is my younger brother, Swarna Mathur. I believe you have already met the rest of the family."

"Yes, sir."

"How can we help you?"

Shankar had decided not to beat around the bush anymore. He decided to put all the cards on the table. In any case, if Rajesh had gone abroad, there was no likelihood that he would be back anytime soon. Nor was there any evidence or witnesses to charge him or the family. Shankar brought out the photograph and placed it on the table for both brothers to see.

He then turned to address Swaroop Mathur.

"I believe, sir, that you worked at the Sahibganj Memorial School before coming to Callipur. You were the facilities manager at the school."

"Yes."

"You knew Professor Saumya Lal and Karan. So did Rajesh."

"Yes." Mr. Mathur's voice had become pensive and worried. Shankar sensed that he was outwardly calm, but his heart must be racing.

"During his time at school, Rajesh was involved with a number of fights with his friends. Some of them were quite serious."

"You know how boys are. They get into scrappy fights."

"Isn't it odd, though, that he was involved in a disproportionate number of them?"

Swaroop Mathur got up immediately. He was angry.

"What does this have to do with anything? Has anyone complained? Are you charging him with anything? We told you that Rajesh was with us on the night of Karan's death. You have our statements."

The loud voice of Mr. Mathur brought both the women back into the room. With the two brothers and their wives in the same room, Shankar decided to let them know what he thought happened that night.

"I am sorry if my questions disturbed you, Mr. Mathur. You are right; we don't have anything to charge Rajesh or the family with. But if you please allow me, I will lay out what I think happened that night. I believe Karan and Rajesh were good friends at school in Sahibganj and Callipur. Rajesh has always suffered from some sort of mental disorder. I am not a doctor, and I can't say with any certainty what that might be. But his condition makes him lose his temper in a violent manner every now and then. He gets into fits of rage, and during such moments, he can hurt himself and those around him. We found out about the incidents in Sahibganj. The school hushed them up with your help. After an incident involving a teacher, they asked you to leave. There have been incidents in the past in other schools as well. That's why you have kept moving. Rajesh has had four schools in the last eight years in three different places. You decided to move to Callipur to be closer to your brother and the hospital, where he had a chance to be treated. Before coming here, I spoke to the principal of Rajesh's school here. He told me that there were some minor incidents here as well but not anything too serious. It seems Karan had stepped in a couple of times to calm Rajesh down and prevent things from escalating. The principal confirmed this." Shankar turned slightly to look at Rita Mathur.

"When I came to speak to Mrs. Mathur to request statements from all of you, the first thing she had asked me was whether Rajesh was in trouble. It didn't strike me as odd at the time, but now it makes sense. There was also an incident at the club a few weeks ago, an altercation with one of the waiters. The club manager smoothed things over with all of you and understandably blamed the waiter and made it sound like a misunderstanding. I was there, but I had failed to make the connection at the time. I think Rajesh probably had one of his episodes, and all of you quickly took him home."

The Mathurs were very quiet, listening to every word Shankar had to say. With each sentence, Nitya could almost sense their anguish and fear. Shankar paused, took a sip of water, and then continued.

"On the night in question, I believe Rajesh went to meet Karan at the garage. Something must have triggered a violent confrontation. I can't say what exactly it was. But I think it may have to do with something Karan had seen in the club with Mrs. Rita Mathur and Pramod Bhaskar. What he saw may have led him to believe that they were having an affair. I checked the phone records, and there were several calls between the auto shop and your residence, including one earlier that evening. I am sure it was not because your car needed service or maintenance that often. It's more likely that Karan and Rajesh spoke to each other as friends, or Mrs. Mathur and Mr. Bhaskar spoke to meet somewhere. It is unlikely that Karan would be using the telephone that often from Mr. Bhaskar's room to call Rajesh without being noticed during work hours. Also, the length of the calls seems to suggest that the reason was probably the latter." Shankar and Nitya could sense that the Mathurs were starting to get agitated.

"I think Karan wanted to ask his friend about the affair when they met up that evening, and that must have made Rajesh angry and lose his temper completely. In a momentary lapse of reason, he struck Karan with a tool that was in the workshop and killed him with a single blow. Then he most likely returned home with the weapon. As always, the rest of his family made sure that all the evidence surrounding the incident was removed or destroyed. You also provided statements to the effect that Rajesh was home all evening. There were no witnesses that saw him go to the auto shop. So, nothing to suggest otherwise."

There was an utter silence in the room, and the Mathurs were completely frozen in time. The pregnant silence was broken by a telephone call, and they quickly recovered their composure. Both Shankar and Nitya knew from their expressions that what had been recited was basically true, even if not entirely accurate. Finally, Swarna Mathur turned to Shankar with a stoic expression.

"This is all speculation at this point. We have already provided our statements and have nothing further to add."

Shankar nodded and looked at them, this time with a calm and pleasing demeanor.

"Yes. You are right. I hope Rajesh gets the treatment he needs to get better. I don't think you can protect him all his life. There will be other outbursts, and you won't always be around to hide his condition. All I can say is that a young man's life was cut short that night. His father died a few weeks ago. There's no one else in his family seeking answers. We will leave now."

Before getting up, Shankar turned to Nitya and asked her, "Is there anything you would like to add or ask?"

"Yes. I am curious, Mr. Mathur. Where is Rajesh studying in England?"

"Imperial College," Mrs. Mathur blurted out before anyone else could say anything. The rest of the family was visibly annoyed with her and then got up.

That was the cue for Nitya and Shankar to leave.

On their way back to the station, Nitya could sense Shankar's disappointment in not being able to convince the family to revise their statements. But she knew that he had done the best he could. Just as she was about to tell him something, Shankar turned to her.

Broken Dreams: A Callipur Murder Mystery

"You know now that as I look back, knowing what we know, many things make sense. Do you remember Karan's cremation? All his friends were standing together, and Rajesh was standing with his own family all around him, probably to manage any sort of outburst. Towards the end, he was crying inconsolably and had to leave early. Even the statements—everyone who corroborated that he was at home were his family members. No one else." Shankar sighed. He was desperately thinking of what he could have done differently.

"You did the best you could with what you knew at the time. Don't beat yourself up. Now, can you please drop me at *The Callipur Post*?"

"Sure."

Once Shankar and Malkhan had dropped Nitya off, they headed back to the station. He wanted to let Maheshwar know what had happened. He was convinced that his boss would be somewhat disappointed.

As he entered the station, he could see that Maheshwar Mishra's office door was shut. His secretary told him that he was in a meeting. But he also informed Shankar that he was to let him know right away when he came back to the station. While Shankar waited outside Maheshwar's office, he could see the secretary go inside and whisper something in his boss's ear. After a few minutes, Maheshwar came out and took Shankar outside to the corridor in a secluded section.

"What happened?"

Shankar quickly recapped what occurred at the Mathur residence. Maheshwar listened without interrupting, all the time glancing up and down the corridor to make sure no one else was listening.

"You did find the truth, Shankar, and that's more than one can say of crimes of this nature. You should be happy about that. I am surprised and extremely pleased with your investigation. Yes, it did not yield the desired result. But given what transpired, it's the best one could hope for."

"But what about Rajesh? He is in England, and we don't really have enough to bring him in."

"I understand. Even if you did, you cannot charge him. If you did find a reason, his family will find enough doctors to certify his mental condition, and anything he may have to say will be inadmissible."

"No justice, then." Shankar was visibly upset.

Maheshwar smiled and looked at him.

"When you have been in the job as long as I have, you will realize that justice takes many forms. I am not sure what it will be in this case. But from what I have heard, it seems these incidents are likely to happen again. Next time around, things may turn out differently for this troubled boy. Of course, one can argue that we ought to be able to prevent this sort of crime with what we now know. But that responsibility is not ours alone, and the police cannot solve all of society's ills."

Shankar nodded in agreement.

"Well, I have to get back to my meeting. Let's talk more this evening. Come to the club, and we will have a drink. And yes—well done."

"Thank you, sir."

As Shankar walked back to his office, he kept thinking about what Maheshwar had just said. Yes, they had solved the case. But there was no sense of justice or closure. Or so it seemed, at least for a while.

11

Diwali

The Colonial Club was always decked out for the festival of lights. This year, the management decided to pull out all the stops. They brought in a live band from Calcutta and a Bollywood singer. The billiard and snooker tables had all been removed on the main floor to make way for a dance floor. They had hired a chef from Delhi to cook some delightful Punjabi food and also roped in someone from a nearby hotel to help them with South Indian cuisine. This was in addition, of course, to the regular fare of local delicacies. The facade had been illuminated from top to bottom with lots of lights. The roof of the club had been cleared of all the plants and decorations. In its place was an open-air bar and lounge. The monsoons were over, and there was no rain in the forecast. Large sections of the garden had been cleared to make way for the fireworks show. The parking lot had also been cordoned off to make sure no cars would be parked there the entire night. The management didn't want to take any chances with cars getting hit with the fireworks.

People started arriving at 6:00 p.m. But most of the crowd showed up around 8:00 p.m. when the bar opened. The invitation said that the festivities would continue until 2:00 a.m. Guests had to leave at the latest by 3:00 a.m. Arrangements had been made with local transportation companies and taxis for any potential stragglers. The guest list, as always, included all the important people in Callipur. Politicians, government officials, industrialists, businessmen, artists—anyone who was someone had been invited. Chairs and sofas had been added to all the rooms, halls, lounges, and gardens to accommodate everyone and their families. The only section of the club that was closed was the library. The club had also arranged for security guards from a private company, in addition to a request to have more police in the area to ward off any untoward incidents.

The guests came in all shapes and sizes. Tall, thin, skinny, fat, overweight—everyone seemed happy. From their attire, one could have mistaken this for the festival of colors. The dresses and saris glittered under the bright lights. Even the men wore traditional Indian attire. It was the one night nothing was taken seriously. Everyone gave themselves and everyone else the right and latitude to party and have a good time.

During all this, one could see different groups forming in sections of the club. This was not by design but by choice. At one end of the club were the old, retired gentlemen drinking and laughing loudly at meaningless jokes. At the other end were their wives, showing off their new, gaudy jewelry and clothes. They were also boasting about how great their sons and daughters were doing in their careers and lives. The laughter emanating from this section of the crowd was usually loud and annoying. The next section and by far the largest, was made up of young families with children. The mothers and fathers were trying to eat, drink, and have a conversation with others at the same time. They were also desperately watching their kids running around, bumping into things, and doing everything to make their parents' evening as chaotic and stressful as possible.

The last section of people were the ones who didn't fit in anywhere else. These were the young people, new to town, those just married or unmarried. They really wanted to be left alone and yet wanted to come to the party. They moved from one section to the other, dodging questions about what they are doing with their lives, when they were getting married, or when they planned to have kids. The aunties looked at this group and were making all sorts of comments that they didn't want to hear. One would have thought that there was almost a competition among them as to whom could make them feel the most uncomfortable with their indelicate remarks.

Broken Dreams: A Callipur Murder Mystery

Despite all this, everyone seemed to be having a great time. The live band had just started playing, and a few people were already on the dance floor. In the early hours, the kids and teenagers usually occupied the floor, along with some old couples. Harsh had arrived early with his son, Akash, who was visiting from Bombay. They had started enjoying the wide variety of food on offer. Maheshwar Mishra was engaged in a deep philosophical conversation with Mr. Shome. He was Judge Shome's husband, and they had found a subject of common interest in ornithology. Gita Shome stayed near her husband for a while, trying to listen to their conversation, but was soon bored out of her brains. She decided to try some of the food and headed towards the food stalls. She ran into Harsh and Akash. They smiled and exchanged pleasantries.

The judge had grown to like Harsh. The young lawyer had turned out to be a formidable attorney and wasn't afraid to take on landmark cases. Even though he had ended up on the losing side on many occasions, the judge was always impressed with his legal prowess and demeanor. She missed work, and retirement had not been kind to her. She had tried painting and picking up the piano, which she had learned as a child. However, she was getting bored. Having her husband at home as well did not help matters. His friends would constantly show up to play cards and talk about meaningless things. That's what old men did; she knew that. But she couldn't stand it beyond a certain point. Lately, she had insisted that he go to the club, which had helped matters somewhat.

As she turned around to pick up a plate and stand in line for the buffet, the woman in front of her turned around.

"Good evening, Mrs. Shome. How are you?"

It took Judge Shome a moment before she could place her.

"Oh, hello, Mrs. Chaturvedi. I am fine, thank you."

"How is Mr. Shome? I see him in the club very often nowadays, but not you."

"Yes." She sighed.

"You should come more often. We have all kinds of events and parties, and we would love it if you came."

"Thank you. I will most certainly make an effort."

The woman in front of Mrs. Chaturvedi then turned around to see whom her mother was talking to. Gita Shome recognized Nitya immediately and smiled at her.

"Hi, Judge Shome."

"Hello, Nitya."

As the line kept moving, there wasn't much by way of conversation, but Mrs. Chaturvedi was adamant to let the judge know about Nitya and Raj. She was convinced that if more people knew about Nitya and Raj, the sooner they would get married.

"Our Nitya will be engaged to Raj soon." She assumed that the judge would automatically know who Raj was, but she didn't. She also didn't want to ask. Any attempt at trying to prolong a conversation with Mrs. Chaturvedi would be self-defeating. But Mrs. Chaturvedi continued.

"Nitya works at *The Callipur Post*."

"I know. I have read her articles. She is a good journalist. I hope she continues working after her engagement and marriage," Gita Shome said.

Mrs. Chaturvedi was visibly annoyed by this remark, and her body language reflected her outright hostility at this point. She turned around, stopped talking to the judge, and continued getting her food. Nitya had overheard the conversation and couldn't help but laugh.

Gita Shome was quick to notice the change in Mrs. Chaturvedi's demeanor. As they headed back with their plates full of food, the judge smiled at Mrs. Chaturvedi and wished her a happy Diwali. Mrs. Chaturvedi acknowledged her with some sort of noisy grunt and a forced smile. She was well on her way to speak to Raj's mom about what had happened and complain about the judge's uncouth behavior.

Meanwhile, the judge wanted to see if she could find Harsh. Conversations with lawyers were much easier now that she had retired and was no longer on the bench.

Nitya headed to find Raj. Her mom had insisted that they come to the party together, and she had made quite a scene at home. Nitya had relented for the sake of keeping peace at home, and Raj had picked her up earlier in the evening. He was in good spirits. He had recently gotten a promotion and wanted to talk to Nitya about their future. Although their moms had talked about their wedding for what seemed to be years, Nitya and Raj had never had a serious conversation about it. It was time. They had decided to talk about it after Diwali. Their moms knew and had, for the most part, decided to leave them alone until then.

Nitya also glanced at the two entrances, looking for Shankar. In the weeks leading up to Diwali, they had bumped into each other at the club library a few times. She also recalled their eventful trip to Sahibganj that had led them to solve the case. A couple of months had passed since then. She had fond memories from that trip. It was only for a day, but sometimes she found herself wondering about the case and the people around the set of events that had unfolded.

She found Raj. He was talking to some of the other managers from the company. They all knew who Nitya was.

Just as they were settling into their chairs for food, there was a blaring announcement that the band would be taking a break, but music would still continue on the club's spanking new music system. It was a gift from one of the sponsors, the owners of the new cement plant that the chief minister had opened. Nitya noticed that young Dr. Daphader and his wife were at the next table. She looked at them and smiled. They waved at her to come over, and she indicated via some atrocious hand gestures that she would after their meal.

Still no sign of Shankar. Maybe he had decided to skip this year's celebration. She saw Maheshwar Mishra seated a few tables away and decided that she would go ask him about Shankar's whereabouts.

The brilliant assortment of food was an assault on all the senses. Diwali didn't just mean good food but lots of it. Once the guests had finished dinner, out came the desserts, and there was no end to the sweets, chocolates, fruits, cakes, and other sugary assortments.

Nitya and Raj decided to take a break from eating and headed over to the doctor and his wife. Dr. Daphader wished Nitya and Raj a happy Diwali. Raj had met the doctor and his wife in the club a few times and quite liked them. Nitya hadn't had much of a conversation with Mrs. Daphader. But she seemed nice and had a pleasant disposition.

"Nice party. Great music," Raj said, forcing the conversation.

"Yes," Smita Daphader replied.

"You had gone to Delhi for a few days?" Nitya asked.

"Yes. We went there for a couple of weeks to visit my parents and in-laws."

"Did you have a good time?"

"Yes. But we are glad to be back." Smita sounded relieved. Nitya didn't press any further.

Broken Dreams: A Callipur Murder Mystery

Raj and the doctor were engaged in conversation around the new cement plant. They also had a common interest in fishing. *Utterly boring*, Nitya thought, and she could see from Smita's reaction that she thought the same. The conversation switched to cricket and the upcoming test match series between India and England next year, then to Bollywood movies. That's when all of them joined in.

As they started talking about the latest cinematic fare, a familiar voice appeared from nowhere and said, "Happy Diwali."

"Shankar!" both Nitya and Dr. Daphader said in unison, happy to see him.

"Where have you been hiding?" the doctor asked.

"I got held up at work."

"Please don't tell me you are on duty."

"Not at all. As you can see, I am not in uniform."

"You look great in that attire," Smita commented. "I really like the color of your sherwani. I have been asking Rohit to wear one for years now, and he simply refuses."

"Not everyone looks as dashing in uniforms and attires as Mr. Sen," her husband said.

Nitya wanted to say something, too, but held back. She wanted to let him know that he looked radiant and wanted to talk to him about a new article she was writing on the industries in Callipur dumping waste into the Bay of Bengal.

"So, Shankar, whatever happened to that boy whose case files I reviewed? I understand fully if you don't want to or cannot talk about it. But I am curious from a medical and purely academic standpoint as to where things stand with his treatment."

"Which young boy?" the doctor's wife asked.

"Rajesh Mathur," Shankar replied and continued. "No, I can definitely talk about the case now."

"Is this connected to what Nitya was working on? The professor's boy who was murdered and the gang of robbers?" Raj asked.

"Yes, the very same." Nitya nodded.

As they were talking, Harsh showed up, smiled at all of them, and listened in. He already knew what had happened in the case. Shankar started speaking.

"The good doctor helped us with the case immensely. We came to him with poorly written case files surrounding the boy's medical history. He was kind enough to confirm that he indeed suffered from a medical condition."

"Unfortunately, there isn't much research in this area going on in India at the moment. But from reading the medical journals and research papers, it seems that he has a mental condition along the lines of something that might be called bipolar disorder. The fits of rage, uncontrollable temper, and bouts of depression all point to that condition. Of course, I am not an expert in that area. I had recommended that he see a specialist in this area right away," the doctor explained.

"Sadly, Doctor, that won't happen. Rajesh died a few weeks ago in a mental institution in Shimla."

"Oh my God! Do you know what happened?" Dr. Daphader asked.

"Not exactly. It was being treated as an accident, or it could have been suicide. I can't say for sure."

Raj turned to Nitya. "Didn't you tell me that he had left for England to pursue higher studies?"

"Yes."

"Nitya had found out that was not the case," Shankar replied.

It was Nitya's turn to speak.

"I contacted the college via a newspaper reporter in London that I had corresponded in the past. He telegrammed me in a week or so that there was no record of any Rajesh Mathur enrolled in Imperial College. Then I figured he must be getting treated somewhere in India or abroad. I made a list with the help of the good doctor here of all the mental institutions in India first. After calling a few of them, I confirmed that he was indeed admitted at the institute in Shimla. I didn't know of his death. Shankar informed us a few weeks ago."

"It wasn't in the papers," Raj said.

"It wouldn't be in Callipur. It was in the papers in Shimla," Nitya replied.

"Yes," Shankar said. "Once I learned from Nitya that he was in Shimla, I had one of my colleagues keep me posted on his treatment. He was the one who informed me of his passing."

Smita had been listening to the conversation quietly and finally broke her silence.

"Nitya, what led you to believe that he hadn't left India for higher studies?"

"Monsoon," Nitya replied.

"I don't understand."

"Most courses in England start in September. When Shankar and I met the Mathurs, they told us that Rajesh had already left India a few weeks ago. That was in early July. It didn't make any sense. I can understand if someone leaves in July or August for courses starting in September, but how likely is it that they would be leaving in May or June? That's what bothered me, and I started checking."

"Nice catch, Nitya. You are a good reporter," Smita said with a smile.

"Yes. She is," Shankar said.

"The case is officially closed, then?" Raj asked.

"Officially, it has been closed for a while. The official line was that the gang of robbers was responsible for Karan Lal's death," Shankar responded.

Harsh had been completely silent in the background. He finally spoke. "The Mathurs have left Callipur. They felt that there were too many prying eyes and rumors, and a new start would help."

"I hope it does and they find some peace, wherever they are," the doctor replied. "This sort of condition puts immense pressure on the family, and it's extremely stressful all the time."

Raj's colleagues were waving at him from afar. He excused himself to go talk to them. Meanwhile, Smita had been summoned by some of her friends at the club to inquire about the handsome policeman that everyone in her group was listening to. She left and sat down with them in a sofa at the edge of the garden, desperately trying to switch topics to something else.

Dr. Daphader left to talk to his new boss at the hospital. He had accepted a permanent position at the institute. He was no longer moving to Delhi to take up his father in-law's practice. That had become a cause of some friction and consternation during their most recent visit to Delhi. He and Smita were happy to be back in Callipur, and Smita had taken up a new job at the club, managing various events and helping in the library. She had made a good circle of friends quickly.

That left Harsh, Nitya, and Shankar together, all enjoying their drinks after dinner. Harsh broke the silence.

Broken Dreams: A Callipur Murder Mystery

"Rajesh Mathur's death. Is that some sort of divine justice, you think?"

"Well, you are the lawyer, Harsh. What do you think?" Nitya asked.

"Honestly, I don't know what to think anymore. The more I deal with cases and legal issues, the less I think it has anything to do with justice."

"What about you, Shankar?" Nitya asked.

"Justice, no. Closure, yes. All I know is that a young man was killed that night. His was an unfinished life, broken dreams. It is hard to say what justice means in cases like this. Maybe you are right, Harsh. I think we should focus more on trying to find the truth. Justice is definitely more elusive."

"Wow," Nitya responded with a smile. "You guys are really philosophical today." They all smiled.

"By the way, I wanted to let you know that I will be leaving Callipur in a few weeks. I have accepted a position in Bombay with another law firm. That way, I will be closer to Akash, and I can see him more often."

"Does Rohini know?" Nitya asked. Shankar knew Nitya was asking about Harsh's ex-wife.

"Yes. She is fine with it. She is happy with her husband, and she told Akash that it was a good idea to have me in the same city."

"I am happy for you," Shankar said. Nitya nodded in agreement. She turned to Shankar.

"What about you, Shankar? When all this started, you told us that you had asked Maheshwar Mishra for a transfer."

"Yes. I had."

"And where does that stand?" Nitya was desperately hoping that the request was rejected and that Shankar wouldn't be going anywhere.

"It came through last week," he said. "I have to join almost immediately. In fact, I am leaving for Delhi soon."

"Wow, that's fast for a government machinery that moves at a snail's pace," Harsh said, sounding surprised.

"So, when will you be leaving?" Nitya asked. Her voice had changed. She suddenly realized that she would miss Shankar immensely, and the thought made her very sad.

"This weekend. My train's on Saturday." That was in two days.

"I will miss both of you, you know," Nitya said, regaining some of her composure to smile with a tinge of sadness.

"I will miss you, too. I thought I wouldn't feel this way, but a part of me will miss Callipur as well," Shankar replied.

Harsh turned to both of them and said, "This was a sad case, really. But what I liked about it is that I met some interesting people that I never knew existed in this town. The two of you, the good doctor."

"Very true," Shankar said.

Akash called out to Harsh. "Dad, you will be missing the fireworks. Let's go outside."

Harsh wished Shankar well, gave him a hug, and told him to keep in touch. Then he and Akash walked towards the end of the garden to find a good place to watch the fireworks display.

"I want to come and see you off at the station," Nitya said, not looking at Shankar. Her voice had suddenly become sad again.

"Sure, Nitya. I must get going now. I need to start packing. I think your mom is looking for you."

Shankar pointed to Mrs. Chaturvedi, who was waving desperately to get her daughter's attention from the other end of the garden. Nitya looked over and sighed. She gestured to her mom that she would be over right away.

"Good night, Nitya, and Happy Diwali. I want to thank you for everything. We wouldn't have been able to solve this case without you. More importantly, I want to wish you the best for your future, whatever you decide to do."

"Thank you, Shankar. I will call you tomorrow. It's the only day we have before you leave."

Nitya turned quickly and started walking towards her mom. She realized that she didn't want to be at the club. She wanted to be left alone. She told her mom that she was heading home. Her mom was worried. She had planned to introduce her and Raj to all her friends who were visiting from out of town.

"I told you, Mom. Raj and I will talk about our future after Diwali. Please don't bother me with all this anymore."

"OK. Please take the car. We will ask Raj's parents to drop us back."

As she turned and walked out of the club, Nitya saw that the fireworks had started. The dark Callipur sky was now bright with the brilliant colors of Diwali. She had to decide whether she was ready to put her future in the hands of someone else's destiny. As she slowly walked towards the car, she realized that she had made up her mind. She looked up at the brilliant sky and smiled.